The Mirror That Is Made

By the same author

Wealden Hill

Storm Light

Thin Reflections
The Mirror That Is Made
All The Colours In A Shade
Once Upon A Chance

Stormwrack

The Chronicles of Jeniche of Antar

Shadow in the Storm

Stealing Into Winter
Exile And Pilgrim
Players Of The Game
Thunder On The Mountain

Daughter of Lighning

In Wake Of The Dead
Dancing With Ghosts
Return To Yesterday

THE MIRROR THAT IS MADE

Graeme K Talboys

Monkey Business

Paperback – ISBN 978-1-909295-15-5
E-Book – ISBN 978-1-909295-16-2

1 2 3 4 5 6 7 8 9 10

Cover design by Graeme K Talboys

Acknowledgements

I would like to thank Rollings Glass in Harrogate for taking the time to explain how mirrors were once made and repaired; Vicky Slowe at the Ruskin Museum, Coniston for useful colour and background information; Alan Wallace, the Administrative Officer at Richmond Park for confirming my distant childhood memories; Munia Khan for kind permission to quote from her work; Pete Brown for his kind words and advice; and Roy Harper for kind permission to use part of the lyrics of his song 'The Same Old Rock' as the title of this book.

Any writer will tell you just how generous other writers, musicians, and artists can be with advice and information. So a big thank you to all my creative friends who took time out from their own projects to enlighten me on all sorts of subjects relevant to this book (and plenty that weren't). Keep creating. Your magic makes the world a better place.

for
all
the
broken

in
body
and
mind

I can’t go back to yesterday
because I was a different person then.
Alice’s Adventures in Wonderland – Lewis Carroll

Setting Up

I'll Buy That Dream

Pershore and Sons had been busy when they went in – noise and gossip, a queue at the cash desk – so they had to wait. And, as usual, Charlie wondered why they never saw Mrs Pershore. Or the Sons. Something dreadful, no doubt. There wasn't anyone who didn't have a horror story to tell. She sighed, distracted herself from her own by looking at the half empty shelves, nudging Miranda for no good reason other than to be nudged back. The dark, bentwood chair by the serving counter looked tempting, but she knew that was reserved for old people.

Sad little memories of long gone places and people skittered through her head, running for cover when Miranda said: "You've got the order book, Charlie."

She blinked herself back into the present, to see Mr Pershore's hand held out across the counter.

"Sorry," said Charlie, pulling the little book from her jacket pocket.

"That's the Co-op one."

Charlie looked at it. Blushed. "Wrong pocket."

She put the Co-op order book away and pulled out the little cash book they used for Pershore's. With a nod of his pale balding head, Mr Pershore took it from her, opened it and laid it on the counter. He took off his round spectacles and polished them on the corner of his brown cotton work coat.

"Sent you for the heavy stuff, I see," he said after he'd scanned the list of tinned foods.

"Mum'll be along later for the rationed items," said Miranda. "She also wants to know if you've got any rice."

He looked around his shop, momentarily empty of customers. "Some pudding rice just arrived," he whispered.

Charlie looked round from the magazine rack where she had inevitably come to a stop. They hadn't had a rice pudding for a long time. And never as good as her Nan had made. But that was inevitable with milk rationing. You couldn't waste it on fripperies. They knew Daisy would be sensible, wouldn't waste points on luxuries, much as she might be tempted. Charlie and Miranda had the same thought and after swapping a quick glance of resignation went back to their tasks.

The tins were placed in the shopping bag and the prices written in beside each item on the list. Miranda had the money so she would have to drag the bag along to the girl at the till and pay. Charlie could hear the tins clatter whilst she was searching the rack, the sound fading from consciousness as she first be-came immersed and then worried. If you didn't get there in time, and this morning they were later than usual, you could sometimes miss out.

In the end she moved every single magazine and newspaper and finally found what she was looking for. Sexton Blake Library Number 94, the latest edition. It had a wonderful cover of a speeding train with murder being committed in silhouette in one of the carriage windows. *At Sixty M.P.H.* it was titled, by John Drummond. Clutching it, she headed for the till. Miranda waited near the door, staring through the window. At least the weather was improving.

Charlie stood at the cash desk separating her pennies and half-pennies from pocket fluff, string, old screws, empty sweet wrappers, a spring clip she thought she had lost, and sundry other items, counting out a total of six-pence ha'penny on the counter by the till. While she was doing this, a young woman hurried in, tears on her cheeks. She managed a contemptuous look for the ragamuffin at the counter, glanced round to make sure Mr Pershore was nowhere to be seen, and leaned across to the girl behind the till.

"It's all over, Sal," hissed the young woman.

"Eh? What is? If Mr Pershore catches me gossiping… Is it you and that Michael? Has he give you the shove? I warned you 'e was no good."

"What? No. The war. Germany gave up. It's all over. In Europe anyway."

"Are you sure?"

"Course I am. I just had it from Elsie what works at the town hall."

"Aren't they supposed to ring the church bells or something? Where's the bells?"

A long, deep silence fell. Charlie listened. She understood the words but it took an infinitely long few seconds before they hit home. Out of nowhere. Like a V2. She put the last ha'penny on the counter and waved her Sexton Blake, before turning to look for Miranda.

Miranda, leaning somewhat exaggeratedly to one side under the weight of a full shopping bag she was meant to be sharing, stood by the door and glared back at her. Speechless, Charlie pulled one of the handles out of Miranda's grasp and then towed her out onto the pavement. Before Miranda had a chance to untangle herself, Charlie was steaming homeward.

"Wait," called Miranda, the heavy shopping bag stretched out between them.

"Come on, Em."

"What's the hurry?"

Charlie stopped. "Didn't you hear?"

"What?" Miranda looked alarmed, peering up the sky.

"No. Not that. Not ever again."

"Eh?"

"The war's over."

"But…" Miranda stared at her wide-eyed. "You're not making it up?"

"Would I? I heard them talking in Pershore's. We have to get home. Listen to the radio."

Even in their excitement they managed to do the big hopscotch grid at the top of the road, the bag of tins swaying back and forth, laying down bruises on both their shins.

At the house, they banged in through the front gate and left it swinging as they raced up the path at the side, leaping Beth's bike where it lay abandoned. The back garden was quiet, no one in sight. They stopped at the back door for a few seconds to get their breath and then stepped inside.

The house was as quiet as the garden. It was eerie and even Charlie, more than used to such situations, shivered. Because this was different. This was her own world, her safe world, the world where she had finally found a new home.

With a fast beating heart and an almost painful tingle in her stomach, she followed Miranda into the kitchen.

As always, the clock ticked steadily. All else was silent, even Daisy who was sitting at the large table, head resting on arms folded over the ration books. They stopped just inside the doorway not daring to speak. Daisy straightened herself, eyes red with tears.

"Is it true, Mum?" asked Miranda in a voice so small it could barely be heard above the clock.

Daisy stood and stepped across the room, gathering them both in a tight embrace.

"It's not been on the radio, but Mrs Smith popped by to tell me. She heard it from her boy."

Mrs Smith's 'boy' was fifteen stone of police constable who stood six foot two inches tall before he put his helmet on. If anyone knew for certain, he would.

Daisy let them both breathe. "The fighting might be over. In Europe, anyway. But it's been a long show. Pulling down will take time. Your father and the others won't be back for a while, Em." She looked at Charlie, brushed hair from her face. "Some of us won't be getting anyone back." She kissed Charlie on the head.

I Can't Begin to Tell You

After the crash, a cloud of dust billowed through the door followed by Beth who stood covered in dirt and soot. The other three turned to watch her.

"You all right?" asked Mary.

Beth coughed, brushed an ancient cobweb from her face, and looked down at her coat. "Daisy is going to skin me alive."

"No she won't," said Charlie. "Give us your coat."

Gingerly, Beth took it off and handed it over. Miranda and Charlie took it between them and gave it a rigorous shake, spreading the dust over all of them.

With a grin, Charlie handed back Beth's coat. "She'll have to skin us all now."

"Idiot," said Mary and laughed.

As Beth heaved her coat back on over the hand-me-down dungarees that were at least three sizes too big, a beetle fell out of her hair. They watched it scuttle away.

"Come on Beetle," said Mary to Beth.

Beth stuck her tongue and instantly regretted it, getting a taste of the sour dust and soot that caked her lips.

A piercing whistle froze them into silence. They looked at each other. Charlie was nearest the front of the room and found herself being pushed to go and see who it was. With a quick glare at the others and an inward shiver at the memories, she picked her way over the rotten floor to a sagging open space that was once a window.

From the shadow to one side she was able to peer out onto the street. Old Tom peered straight back in at her with a wicked grin on his face. Stepping back, Charlie put her foot through a rotten board and sat down with a thump.

"Get yourselves out of there," called Tom. "You're making noise and dust enough for a whole troop of monkeys."

Tom waited out on the pavement. The four girls clambered out through the planks nailed criss-cross over the doorway.

"What we were you doin in there, anyway? Those houses ain't safe. You all know that. And look at the state of yer. Bunch of scarecrows if ever I saw one."

"Did you?" asked Beth.

"A little less of your lip, young Bethany Tennant. Or is it Beetle now?"

She came as close to stamping her foot as she ever had, settled for glaring instead, knowing the name was going to stick.

Tom narrowed his eyes, barely suppressing his smile. "Well?"

"We were looking for stuff for the bonfire," said Charlie.

"Bonfire?"

The girls exchanged glances.

"Didn't you know?" asked Miranda.

"What's that?"

"The war. The Germans have given up. It's over."

He screwed up his mouth to hold back the tears, his hands slowly clenching and unclenching until he pushed them into his trouser pockets. The girls looked on in silence. They knew he'd been in France during the first war, although he rarely said anything about it. "Been in the warehouse all morning," he croaked.

Clearing his throat, he turned away.

"Best be getting that cart of yours out of there and across to the warehouse." He added as he turned and started to shuffle away.

By the time they'd manoeuvred the cart out of the alley and put back all the bits that had dropped off, the street was deserted. Nobody said anything as they guided the old pram chassis down the hill and across to the open door of the warehouse. They all walked with their coats open and flapping, looking like the crows Tom thought they'd scare. It had been cool and wet the previous few days but it was getting warmer and they all wished they'd left their coats at home.

In the gloomy space of the warehouse with its cocooned fairground rides, they could hear Tom clattering about somewhere near the raised office. It had been a long time after Alice died before he'd felt comfortable returning there on his own.

They made their way across between the tarpaulin covered stacks, pushing the cart.

Tom smiled at them out of the shadows. "Hang them coats on the rail." He pointed with a thumb.

There were four wooden coat hangers suspended from one of the metal stanchions. While they took their coats off, Tom produced a carpet beater.

"Give 'em a good whack and when you've done, get yourselves up the far end. Big pile of rubbish up there. Just right for a bonfire."

By the time they'd carted the final load down to the bomb site, it was late afternoon. They had barely sneaked in through the back door before Daisy appeared at the kitchen doorway, her arms crossed.

"Bath. The lot of you. Now."

In tired, giggly silence they kicked off their plimsolls and hauled themselves upstairs, aware of Daisy inspecting their coats on the long rack in the back hall.

A semblance of cleanliness was achieved sufficient for Daisy to allow them to sit at the kitchen table with all the other younger members of the family to eat their tea. It was a noisy meal. The prospect of peace was secondary in their minds to the prospect of a huge bonfire. As they finished and cleared away, Daisy oversaw cooked food for the adults who would soon be returning home from work.

Plates and cups were gathered, washed, dried, and put away in a whirlwind that even now left her surprised that everything made it to its place in the cupboards in one piece. And then the whirlwind left, followed by the usual futile warning to behave.

Strange Things Happening Every Day

Even as dusk fell, debris kept appearing. How so much had survived the long, cold years of war was anyone's guess. Yet there was no way they were going to wait for some official celebration. A number of people in the surrounding streets had shut up their houses and made their way into the city centre, to Buckingham Palace mostly, in hope of some official benediction. Others had hung out faded, ragged bunting.

But these were not, on the whole, streets populated by those who toadied to authority. They had looked after themselves during the last six years, helped each other, seen off the chancers and looters without expecting or asking for help from the police or anyone else.

It was the same on the bombsite. There had been no meetings, but there were men there of all ages marshalling the arrivals of material for the bonfire and then organising the building of an enormous pile. When Charlie and Miranda arrived with Beth and Mary, they were greeted with a cheery wave from an older man in a coat and muffler.

"Run out of stuff?" he asked.

Before they could answer, two boys were led away by the ear, howling.

"Little so-and-sos from Kitchener Street rolled up here with someone's front door," said the old man. "Not seen anything of Tom, today. He all right?"

"He was sorting out all the stuff we brought along," said Beth. "He said he might be down later when he's had his tea."

"Right you are. If you see him first, tell him George has a bottle of the good stuff he kept safe to share tonight."

They wandered onto the site. It had once been a terrace of houses, long since bombed and bulldozed flat. Now it was filling with people, mostly young as yet, milling about in a subdued way. Groups gathered and chatted, people wandering away to join other groups and conversations. There was some laughter, but it was gentle.

The darker it grew, the more adults appeared, often in a semi-dazed condition. They also congregated, gathering in their own children.

When the fire was finally lit there was a cheer from everyone there. Someone called out "Put that bloody light out." Someone else yelled, "Never again, mate. Never again."

Mary and Beth wandered off to see who was playing a gramophone and watch the couples who were dancing.

Charlie and Miranda stood side by side watching as the flames worked their way up the huge pile of wood. Charlie shuddered, watching the whole city burn, and felt Miranda take her hand, pulling her back into the here and now.

"Are you all right?" asked Miranda, alarmed by the way Charlie had jumped.

"I…"

What could she say? That two boys chasing through the crowd had gone straight into the bonfire and no one had noticed. That now she was alert to the fact, a group of girls were skipping in the same place as the couples who were dancing, passing through them wholly unconcerned. That a small child in muffler, balaclava, and fingerless mitts had winked at her as she passed.

"Did you not see…?"

And jumped again at the sudden series of explosions. A woman screamed.

The ghosts vanished and Charlie stood gasping for breath with Miranda looking on not knowing what to do.

Adults were arguing.

"It's only some bloody fireworks."

"Bit soon, mate. People here were bombed out."

"Save 'em for November. Be better then."

There was grumbling, but there were no more fireworks.

"Charlie?"

She didn't respond. Miranda shook her arm gently.

"Charlie?"

Charlie's eyes came back into focus, homed in on Miranda's face, lit by roaring firelight. She took a deep breath and let it out in ragged blasts.

"Sorry, Em. Don't be scared."

"You were." She sounded half angry.

There was no answer to that.

"You didn't see them?"

"What?"

Charlie took another deep breath. Where could she possibly begin?

Blues At Sunrise

It was getting on for eight months since Charlie had moved into the Simmons' house, shared a room with Miranda, shared a bed through the cold winter, yet she still woke in the night expecting to see the cellar where she had lived for several years; its high window, stone floor, spider haunted lavatory across the corridor, the steps up to the courtyard where she had grown her vegetables.

She lay and stared across to where Miranda slept, just visible in the darkened room, a wisp of honey coloured hair emerging from beneath the devastation of blankets. Books were piled everywhere, especially on the old school desk. On her own dresser, squeezed in behind the door, a spindly Victorian chess set lay in a heap awaiting repairs and a board, reflected in the old speckled mirror. She wiggled her toes in the comfortable warmth, happier than she had been in a long time. Here with her best friend, surrounded by people who, for the most part, accepted her as family, even though she was a stranger. Free now, for a while, of the nightmares.

Yet.

It still felt too good to be true. Something she did not deserve. A severing of ties she did not want broken. Like a dream someone else was dreaming, a dream she was permanently frightened would end. Like her lies and deeds would be found out… And now the war was nearly over and everything would change again.

All the pieces that seemed fixed were loose once more, rattling in the box. Perhaps the ghosts would go now. She shivered. One ghost, forever frozen in the grim and icy waters of the bombed cellar would never be gone. It might not be haunting her sleep for now, nightmares difficult to explain when they woke the person you shared a room with, but he still stalked her, still lurched with no warning out of daylight shadows.

Till The End Of Time

Sudden, hard light filled the skylights and made the cocoons in the warehouse jump sideways. Tom and Charlie peered out from their pool of warm lamplight for a moment. As thunder rattled the roof, Tom leaned sideways and with the gentlest of touches, retuned the wireless set to get back the music. He wasn't worried about that so much as missing the news. Several of the men from the fair were still out East and he liked to know what was happening.

On the long table in front of them were laid out all the parts of the organ from the gallopers that had once belonged to Alice. Tom had tried to explain who the ride passed to, but the Simmons family was nothing if not complex and there was, besides, something of a dispute going on. In the end it would come down to Tom to decide.

"I'm too tired for that sort of thing," he'd said at the end of his explanation. "Whoever I pick, someone else is going to feel left out. Or hard done by. And the last thing we need now we can get back on the road is bad feeling."

"Couldn't it just belong to the whole family? To the fair?"

Tom put down the complicated wooden crank shaft he had been cleaning. Charlie wilted a bit under his stare as his eyes narrowed. He muttered something about paperwork and then nodded as if it was all settled.

"And what about you?" he asked. "How you gettin' on? I know Alice would've asked before now. I ain't so good at that sort of thing."

Something must have shown in her face. She didn't even begin to know how to put it into words. That she loved having a home, loved sharing a room with Miranda, loved being able to be clean and warm and fed, loved not living in fear the whole time. That she found it all so stifling she could scream.

And then there was the one thing she couldn't ever tell Tom, that she hadn't even yet told Miranda, the thing that might kill the dream stone dead.

"Don't worry about it," he said. "It's not easy going home after all that time fighting. 'Specially when it ain't even yer own home. Which isn't to say you aren't welcome. You're family, make no mistake."

"I love it, Tom. I feel as safe and wanted here as I ever did with my Mum and my Nan."

"But…?"

A tear sprang hot in the corner of her left eye.

"Now, now," he said. "Don't take on so. You can always escape out here. There's always gonna be stuff needs doing to the machinery. You seem to have the knack for it. And as you get older, you'll p'raps be wanting a pitch of your own."

Charlie's eyes flicked to the tarpaulin in the corner where Tom kept the motorbike he had restored. She sighed. He pretended not to notice.

"Anyway, that's all a long way off. You got to take time to catch up on things. Can't have been any fun living like you did. And not one in a thousand adults could've done what you done. But just remember, whatever you do, you are always welcome in the house and you are always welcome here."

Charlie scrubbed the tear away and made herself smile. Tom watched her for a moment more. He'd had no children of his own and he didn't talk much unless it was about the fair. He decided that a word with Daisy would be in order.

"And look at me," he added. "Twenty-seven year since I come home and I still can't settle." He too wiped away a tear.

Charlie picked up another of the brass pipes and threaded the cleaning brush along its length. Music played on the wireless set. More thunder rumbled in from a distance. A voice mumbled on the wireless and Tom reached out once more, this time to turn up the volume so he could listen to the news.

> "...first atomic bomb has been dropped on the Japanese city of Hiroshima from a United States aircraft. The new type of bomb was, said a spokesman, two thousand times more powerful than the largest bomb so far used."

"And it seems we're still doing it to each other," Tom said, mostly to himself.

> "...dropped at 08:15 local time from an American B-29 Superfortress called *Enola Gay*. The crew of the plane say they saw a column of smoke rise above the city as intense fires spread. Further observation has been impossible because of a thick cloud of dust hanging over the city.
>
> "President Harry S Truman, speaking from the *USS Augusta* in the mid-Atlantic, said the new bomb was 'harnessing the basic power of the universe'."

"There's been a lot of talk these last years about the future," said Tom. "Making things better, more equal, schools for all, doctors for all, that sort of thing. Avoiding the bad things that happened after the last go. A land fit for heroes. That's what they promised us when we come back in 'nineteen. Didn't happen, though. And the fear is it won't happen again. Too many folk with their grubby fingers in the till don't want it to happen lest they lose out while things get better for others.

> "'...expect a rain of ruin from the air the like of which has never been seen on Earth.'"

"Vicious bastards, pardon my French. Grasping, greedy, and with an inbred hatred of the common people. They're every bit as violent as the street corner thug they employ for their dirty work."

> "'The possession of these powers by the Germans at any time might have altered the result of the war.'"

"And the people themselves?"

He sighed.

"Send them to fight wars and they have the hearts of lions. Ask them to stand up to the bosses at home, they'll maybe moan a bit about how bad their lives are and then find any old excuse to stay prone in the dirt while their bosses grind their faces with the heel of their expensive, hand made boots"

> "'...pray that these awful agencies will be made to conduce peace among the nations and that instead of wreaking measureless havoc upon the entire globe they become a perennial fountain of world prosperity.'"

He looked at Charlie's bewildered expression.

"Sorry about that. Been a long day. And now this bomb. It's not your burden." And under his breath, so quiet she did not hear, he added, "Not yet."

Ich Will Kein Engel Sein

Day By Day

Snow fell on the dead.

Broad flecks of white sifting downward from the leaden sky, settling flake by silent flake along the dark, broken tracery of branches, piling ever higher along the tops of the headstones, clinging to the carvings and statuary in sagging drifts, carpeting the ground with deepest silence.

Nothing moved but the snow, twisting in flurries, carried on breezes too weak to stir the branches. And into the silence a muffled whirr of wheels, a vortex of flakes spinning in the wake of the speeding rider.

There were no gates any more, no railings. The old bicycle with its time-scarred silver paint whispered unhindered between the stone pillars and past the long-deserted gatekeeper's lodge, following a route so familiar it little mattered that it was hidden beneath a thick layer of snow. Bundled in layers of khaki buttoned tight over layers of wool, her head encased in a balaclava and scarf, Charlie steered to the right, following a side path beneath trees and past crumbling Victorian memorials, before emerging on the edge of the vast circular field. Row upon row of irregular slabs stood dark against the stark whiteness of the world.

A shiver climbed her spine as it always did, but she pushed on, ploughing along the broad path across the centre of the circle, puffing out clouds of steam. Snow drove into her face and she blinked the freezing points of softness from her eyes.

On the far side, she dismounted. Her feet squeaked in the new snow as she pushed the bike along a narrower path toward a hedge. Leaning it against the cold foliage, she brushed away the snow that slid off and then shrugged. If it didn't stop snowing, the bike would be covered anyway by the time she returned.

Happy that the padlock key was safe back inside her glove, she pushed through the gap in the hedge to the small section beyond. Snow had drifted there and she kicked through, clapping her hands to knock the icy crust from the wool of her gloves and to warm her hands.

"I didn't bring flowers, Nan." she said as she bent to push snow from the stone pillow. "Em said you'd understand. Em knows what she's talking about."

The wool of the back of her glove was rough against her face as she rubbed away the tears.

"What am I supposed to do, Nan? What am I supposed to do? Is Mum still alive?"

She looked up, stared at the snow, thought she saw a still figure in the far distance. Snow flicked into her eyes and by the time she had blinked it away, the figure was gone. Charlie shivered again, telling herself it was just the cold.

Just for once, she thought, it would be good to have a decision made for her. But it had been years since she'd had that luxury. And even then it was simple day-to-day survival. Do this and live. Do that and die. Now it was complicated, laying down criss-crossing tracks that stretched into a future she could not see. All those years she had been able to step sideways into other worlds, see other pasts and other futures, and now everywhere she looked was as blank as the cemetery around her. Cold, silent, no way of knowing, no footprints to guide her except her own leading back the way she had come.

And perhaps that was her answer. She sighed. Perhaps. If it had just been left alone. Day-to-day.

She knew Old Tom had meant well. And all the others he must have discussed it with. Daisy. Perhaps even Em's father. He'd been home for Christmas. Was gone back to Germany, still not knowing when he'd be demobbed.

"At least the poor bastards'll have somewhere warm to have their nightmares," she'd overheard him say.

Give Me Five Minutes More

The day had started with magic. Miranda had bounced out of bed, dragged on a coat and wellingtons and pulled Charlie after her so they could go and catch snowflakes on their tongues. Mary and Beth had ambushed them from the old air raid shelter and a furious snowball fight had ensued until they were shouted indoors and told they wouldn't get any breakfast until they were properly washed and dressed.

Once they were stuffed with porridge, which Daisy had laced with precious golden syrup, and had started to clear away, Tom had appeared in the doorway.

"Warehouse in ten minutes?" he'd asked Charlie.

Daisy had pushed her off with a firm hand to wrap up warm. She had her pyjamas on under her dungarees. An extra pullover, fraying at the hem, on top of her indoor one. An old engineer's jacket faded to a pale blue from years of washing, patched at the cuff and the elbows. A scarf. And then Miranda had appeared to helped Charlie struggle into her greatcoat.

By the time she had waddled downstairs, fingerless mitts and a balaclava had been added. If she got covered in snow she'd be mistaken for a snowman. She knew she needed it though. There was no heating in the warehouse.

Which proved how wrong she could be. Tom had put Alice's paraffin heater back in the office and the air was warm and thick with fumes.

"Can't seem to get the wick properly trimmed," he'd muttered as Charlie struggled to undo the buttons on her coat.

"It don't matter, anyway. Won't want to hang around. Just wanted to give you these where you could have a bit of peace and quiet."

Charlie frowned as Tom produced two heavy envelopes. He handed them to her and she looked at them. Her name was written on both. A shiver made her hunch her shoulders. She thought of her mother's letter and all her Nan's papers in her trunk in the house.

"Gone on then, you won't find out what's inside 'less you open them."

She put the thicker of the two down on the trestle table Tom had clearly been using for fairground paperwork. The envelope she held wasn't sealed. With clumsy fingers and a hard beating heart she pulled out the contents and opened up the sheets of paper.

As she read, she could see Tom fidgeting.

"But…"

Charlie read it again. A letter confirming she was now a fully paid up member of the Showmen's Guild of Great Britain.

"I thought they changed the rules. I thought I had to be family. And anyway, I can't afford this."

"One thing at a time, girl. One thing at a time. First year's a gift. Tradition in Simmons. You'll pay your own way from next year if you want to stay. 'Sides, couldn't put you on the payroll till you were a member. And all the work you been doing here, you needs to be on the payroll."

She looked at him with questioning eyes. He pointed at the other envelope.

After folding the first surprise and putting the papers away, she reached for the heftier envelope.

As she read, Tom said: "It ain't finalised. That's up to you. It was enough for the Guild for this year."

Charlie's hand was shaking. "But how can I be?"

"Did some digging. It's all paperwork these days. Certificates and whatnot. You'll need a lot of that stuff in there in any case," he said waving his hand at the thick sheaf of papers Charlie held. "Your Nan probably had insurance, for what it's worth, and a will and things. Em says you kept all that. But the family talked it through. And I found we had some Cornelius's in the family way back when. Not sure it's your lot, just wanted to do the right thing by you."

"I'd have to change my name?" She sounded frightened.

"No. Never. I checked all that. You'd be adopted, part of the family all legal. But you'd be like… a distant cousin. Keep your name and everything. All official. Not unusual since the war. See?" He pointed a finger at all the paperwork again. "Charlotte Jennifer Grace Cornelius on everything."

Prisoner Of Love

There were no answers to her questions from her Nan. No answers from any of the dead and none she dared face just now from the living. The whole world was silent, enveloped in a deadly, grey cold that swirled thickly about her.

It grew darker, distance fading and flickering. A deep groan sang low in the air and rumbled like a deep thunder beneath her feet – an infinitely vast and infinitely distant creak of compressed snowfields on the move, broken by a succession of concussions that hurt her frozen ears, moving back and forth as sonorous echoes.

In the haze, the inevitable loomed, a darker presence in the heavy grey as if the snow became denser until it hung solid against the world. Beneath her foot the ice of a puddle creaked and snapped as she slid and stumbled, the surface shattered into broken radial patterns. She stared down, thrown off balance by the feeling she was looking down at a lake from a great height, looking down at a frozen Dal from the mountains by the bungalow.

And then she was standing at the foot of her Nan's grave as the snow stopped for a moment. Standing alone. Not understanding.

There were all these people who actually wanted her to be part of their family. It was a wonderful thing yet, crouched in her mind was the fear that it was some sort of betrayal. The desire to belong was strong, a bright light, a warm embrace that felt as if she was walking away from her Nan, from her mother, abandoning them, letting them grow dim.

It frightened her because so little remained of those who had brought her into the world and loved her. Her memories felt moth-eaten and fragile. A diary written in pencil that was already beginning to fade. A chocolate wrapper. So little else. Not even a photograph.

If she embraced this new future, allowed it to embrace her, how could she stop it swallowing her whole? She thought of Miranda then. And wondered if she wanted to stop it swallowing her whole?

As always she would have to make it up as she went along.

Tired, aching, she knelt in the snow for a moment to touch the hard earth of her Nan's grave. Then, brushing the snow from her knees, she turned away.

Blind to the world, Charlie unchained her bike and pushed it slowly across the field of the dead, slow steps leaving a fresh trail across the snow that she looked back at, snapping in and out of her memory as if seen from a height through a… She shook her head and plodded on. When she reached the far side of the trees, a dark shape detached itself from the cold shadows and began to follow.

Surrender

Charlie was lost in place and thought, confused by echoes reaching back to her from some ice bound future. Beneath a growing accretion of ice, buildings stood, fading behind the glassy facades. Twisted crystalline structures sutured the freezing blocks together, the blue of pure ice dusted with the blazing white of snow.

In both places she was conscious of searching. In that gelid future she sought for a shadow whilst in her present a shadow sought for her, hunting through the wintry streets. Footsteps squeaking in virgin snow, the rattle of the wind, bleak vistas born of tiredness, confusion, the cold, the promise of a door held open for her.

Usually it was enough to pour out her tale to her Nan. The very act of unburdening herself was palliative and allowed her to step back and think through the problem for herself. This time, however, the cold had echoed intact the maze of her thoughts; a starveling reflection.

She wandered the palace of ice that built itself around her, dismayed at her own distress. She had been freely offered all that she could desire and it frightened her. A settled future was something she had never thought to experience, no matter how often she had dreamt it.

As a very young child she had lived always in the here and now under the protection of those who loved her. As an orphan, she had counted each day alive a small victory. Thoughts of a tomorrow were small comforts in substitute for the love in which she had once been warmly embraced.

Day by day was all she really knew, that and a past that was now mythical and increasingly unreachable. It had been rich and safe, the small bungalow and garden in the mountains by the lake, the steamy kitchen with cuddles and laughs.

Tears froze on her cheeks.

She picked them away, heard them shatter as they hit the ground, was distracted by the sound of laughter, a glow of cold light from a shop window around which a group of children had gathered, peering at the toys within.

Philip Flower was the name painted over the window. Charlie frowned. She did not recognise the shop or the street. It frightened her. And the children had gone, laughter from around a nearby corner. She followed, breath clouding the air, a turning pedal catching her shin as she let the bike get too close.

In the grey afternoon light she could see a park in the distance; closer to hand, a pile of rubble overlooking a bomb site where children played silent games.

Tired, cold, Charlie dislodged frozen snow as she leaned her bike against a rickety fence and clambered through a gap. On the other side she made her way up the icy pile of bricks and squatted at the top.

Below, they played, oblivious to the weather, to their mortality, lives snatched away by bombs and burning buildings. It brought a smile to her lips and she rocked slowly back and forth, herself unseeing.

The stone inside the snowball knocked her sideways and she rolled in a cloud of ice crystals, staggering to her feet with warm blood on her face wondering what had happened.

"Loony! Bugger off."

She watched another incoming snowball, still not understanding. It hit her full in the chest and even through the many layers she wore she could feel the heavy stone at its core.

Three of them. By the fence. One of them trying her bike for size whilst the other two yelled at her and bent to cluster more snow round the stones they had gathered. And then, a small, dark, howling fury out of nowhere launched itself at the boy astride the saddle.

Hit full on, he toppled sideways, legs tangled in the bike's frame, screaming with pain as the fury rolled to its feet and launched itself at the other two. By this time, Charlie had begun the climb down the brick slope, blood pouring into her left eye.

The boy tangled in the bike was still howling and the other two had turned on their attacker, putting their backs to Charlie. She vaulted the fence and slithering on packed snow, managed to get an arm round each neck and bring their heads together. Muffled by balaclavas and scarves, it was the surprise more than the pain that put them off balance.

One went down. The other ran.

And Charlie found herself embraced by Miranda.

On the long walk back home, they stopped outside the toy-shop. Charlie had the most abominable headache and wanted to rest for fear of being sick. Miranda stood with her, feverish with the excitement of what she had done, barrelling out of nowhere and bringing down the urchins that had attacked Charlie. Neither of them noticed that the shop was dark.

Miranda produced a clean handkerchief from somewhere deep within her layers of clothing and dabbed gently at the cut on Charlie's forehead.

Charlie watched Miranda's eyes as she worked, knew she was certain, waited until their gazes locked.

"I wanted to know," said Miranda. "Tom told me. About the papers. So I followed you."

"Em." Her throat almost strangled the words before she could say them, so great was her fear. But she had to tell Miranda or live with the never knowing. "I love you. I'm in love with you and have been for months."

And now she stood on the edge of an abyss watching for some sign, more scared than she had ever been, weak to the point of fainting, caught by surprise as Miranda leaned forward and kissed her on the lips with the gentlest, most powerful, magnificent and permanent of kisses. A kiss that was more than she had ever hoped for; a kiss that was all she had ever dreamed of. A kiss that was all the response she needed.

They walked home in silence, hand in hand with a grip so tight it hurt to let go when they finally reached the garden gate. Inside, Daisy separated them from their layers of clothing, sat Miranda by the stove, and fussed over Charlie's cut with cotton wool soaked in TCP.

When Daisy left the room they sat grinning at each other like idiots. Above them they could hear a bath being filled. When Daisy called for Miranda, she stood and then stopped by Charlie on the way out, taking one of her hands in her own.

"Forever," said Miranda. "With all my heart."

And Charlie realised she was looking at a future she could live with.

How Like A Winter

Ain't Nobody Here But Us Chickens

A shadow crept through the early morning gloom of the warehouse, emerging from darkness to cross the floor and fade once more into obscurity. In the stillness that followed, a gentle snore drifted down from the gallery outside the offices. Someone suppressed a snigger. There was a moment's silence and then a second shadow wove its way between the cocoons toward the foot of the stairs.

Another silence followed, long enough this time for recently acquired Record watches to be checked, second hands ticking round to the agreed time. Charlie raced part way up the stairs, her boots lifting dust from the planks, her voice raised: "My God, it's all gone. Stop thief!"

Her shout was followed by the satisfying thud of someone falling off a camp bed. Muffled curses emerged from beneath entangling blankets. A scramble of noise and a voice: "Stop where you are. We can see you!"

It echoed round the warehouse, followed by the snap of an air rifle, the dull thuck as the pellet hit tarpaulin.

"Oi!" yelled Beth from the darkness. "That almost came close to being near!"

"Morning boys," said Charlie as she mounted the final few steps.

Alan stepped back in surprise and fell over his tipped up camp bed. The rifle fell with a clatter and Charlie stepped forward to scoop it up.

"Want to be careful with this," she said.

Alan scrambled to his feet and made a grab at the weapon, but Charlie held it out of reach over the railing. Mary and Beth climbed the stairs and stood beside her.

"Enjoy your sleep boys?" asked Beth.

"Shut up, Beetle," said John.

"Great comeback," said Mary. "You Cutwood toe rags were supposed to be keeping watch."

"What's the point," replied Alan. "No one's tried to break in since that time in February."

"Der," said Charlie. "Cos someone's been in the warehouse every night since then."

"More likely them new doors Tom had fitted."

Charlie looked across the warehouse to the far side at the small doorway where she had first entered this world, at the larger double doors where the fairground lorries came and went. All brand new. Heavy. Bristling with bolts and locks. It seemed like yesterday and yesterday seemed like a whole different world. Who knows, she wondered, where all the time goes?

"Anyway," Alan continued, "who's going to nick fairground machinery?"

"They tried earlier, didn't they? Nick anything these days just for scrap value if nothing else. And they made a right mess before they got chased off. We're still mending stuff, checking stuff is safe that could have been on the road. Didn't do Tom much good either."

There was an uncomfortable silence.

"Better get into breakfast before it spoils otherwise Daisy'll have your guts and hand 'em over for timing belts."

Heartaches

When the shadow fell across her, Charlie let go of the riser she almost had in place and bounced up from the floor only to find it had not been cast by Miranda.

"Expecting someone else? Sorry to disappoint you," said the man standing there, the hint of a smile on his face. "We haven't met properly."

Charlie was wiping her hands on some cotton waste as he spoke. Happy they were clean she offered her right hand. "I'm Charlie. Charlotte. Charlotte Jennifer Grace Cornelius."

The man took her hand and nodded. They shook.

"George Eric Russ."

Charlie's heart was beating hard. This man in his grey flannel trousers and brand new white shirt with the cuffs rolled back twice was Miranda's father. And if everything she had learned about Simmons funfair was true, then this was the man who would eventually take over. The man who would employ her or throw her out. The man whose daughter she loved more than anyone else in the world.

"Are… are you home for good, now?" she asked.

The faint smile turned into a broad grin. "I am."

Charlie wasn't fooled by the grin. True, he was happy to be back, but she knew the scars that waking nightmares etched deep in the soul and the shadows they left in the face.

"And," he added, "I have a lot of catching up to do. Two things first. Thank you for being a friend to Miranda. And I know that Alice gave it to you and that Tom has accepted it, but I need to see your share. These things have to be done by the rules. And, anyway, I'm curious."

"It's in our room."

"I'll wait here."

He was lighting a cigarette as Charlie raced off through the warehouse.

She had seen him before, of course, when he'd been home on leave. Fleeting visits that always left Daisy in the depths of depression when he had gone. Not for herself but for the things her husband had seen and had to deal with.

Charlie had only ever overheard snippets of conversation, one in particular that stuck. She'd nipped back from the warehouse earlier in the year to warm up a bit and get an extra scarf. Passing along the back landing with her boots off, she'd heard his voice. "There were fairground folk in there, Daisy. Along with the Jews, the disabled, the mollys and the dykes, and all the others those bastards thought of as riff-raff, there were fairground folk. Fairground folk. What were they doing in there? What were any of them doing there? What madness? What sickness let that happen?" She had sneaked away when she heard sobbing, extra scarf forgotten.

But she knew about the camps, the wire fences, the trains, the dogs, the shouting and the rifle butts, the long lines of people stripped of everything. Knew about them in a way she could never have explained to anyone.

She raced through the back garden now, saw Daisy at the kitchen window who smiled and waved, pounded up the stairs, and came to a sudden standstill in the tranquil space of the room she shared with Miranda. Stared at the bed not slept in and felt the ache return. They hadn't been apart this long since they met, certainly not since they had grown aware of how deeply entangled they were with one another, how much in love.

For a moment she was lost and buried her face in Em's dressing gown where it hung behind the door; turned her head and saw her reflection in the mirror and thought it a pale, half thing without Miranda there looking out as well.

Then she hauled out her trunk from under her utility bed. Opened the Kashmir biscuit tin, lifted the postcards she'd had from Miranda and found the silver locket with the token inside. Was back out and across the garden before it occurred to Daisy to check that she had taken off her work boots before going into the house.

At the back door to the warehouse she stopped and drew breath, calming herself. When she was breathing normally, she carried her thudding heart slowly into the cool interior.

There were spaces now where some of the pieces of equipment had been broken out of their cocoons and emerged as the bright butterflies of fairground rides. It still seemed strange even after all those months. Charlie couldn't help but associate it with Miranda going on the road. The excitement and then the secret tears when Tom insisted Charlie stay to help with ongoing repairs and checks. She knew she couldn't refuse. She had a way with machinery. As everyone kept reminding her.

Back at the work bench at the far end, Miranda's father stood, peering down at something, right arm loosely at his side, cigarette sending up a thin signal in the still air.

He looked up as she approached and watched as she placed the locket on the bench and unfolded her pocket knife. The edge of the blade turned in the indentation on the side and the locket clicked open. Charlie turned it over above her hand and held out the token that had been concealed within.

George picked it up from her palm and inspected it carefully. Miranda had warned Charlie that her father was not a talkative man. Not like Tom who could talk the hind leg off a donkey and then persuade it to go for a walk. So Charlie waited.

The token was handed back and Charlie shut it away. George held out his hand once more and she passed the locket to him. He gave it the same close scrutiny as he had given the token and finally nodded.

As he gave it back, he said: "The fair is Tom's responsibility for now. He has accepted that you hold a share and therefore have the right, when you come of age, to run your own attraction."

There was a moment of stillness. Charlie did not know George well enough to read him, to understand what he was thinking.

"Tom won't always be in charge," he continued and Charlie had a sinking feeling. "Although nothing is fully settled, it's... complicated. Daisy will probably be head of the family when Tom steps down."

"I thought..."

"That it would be me? No," he replied to her nod. "It's always been the distaff side that owns and runs the fair. That had been Alice. Tom only stepped in during the war. When it comes to it, I'll probably do the bulk of the paperwork, though. Like Tom."

Her throat had gone dry. George went quiet for a moment.

"Not very good at this sort of thing," he said. "Daisy says there may be some who question how you came to have a share."

He held up his hand before she could explain about Alice and the token, uncertain in any case how she could do that.

"Me, I don't care. Alice gave it you. Tom was a witness. Even if you didn't have it, I'd welcome you for your friendship with my daughter. They were both so..."

He seized up with an embarrassed smile on his face and Charlie realised his right hand, free of its cigarette, was thrust out in her direction.

They shook hands again.

"Welcome to the family."

Sugar Blues

When it became too difficult to keep a smile on her face, Charlie slipped out of the kitchen, through the back door and out into the garden. It was pleasantly cool and she stood for a while by the great oak tree. Noise from the kitchen still reached her. The laughter and happy raised voices kept on reminding her that Miranda hadn't come home with the first group and was probably still on the road or stuck in Leatherhead.

Kicking at the long grass at the edge of the lawn, she moved further into the darkness, considered the air raid shelter until she remembered she didn't have the key, and ended up following the familiar route along the paving slabs and round an abandoned bike to the hole in the fence at the back that gave on to the path that led to the rear door of the warehouse.

The desire to sulk dissolved as she entered the dark, reverberant space and made her way between the familiar, ever changing cocoons. Freshly bathed and in what passed for her best clothing, she wandered between the tarpaulin covered mounds, gravitating toward the long stack closest to the raised office. She couldn't be with Miranda, but she could be with her mirrors.

They hadn't been moved since she'd first discovered them all those years ago. All through the war, they'd been stacked there. Reflecting nothing but darkness and, sometimes, the pale face of a child in search of answers.

She'd found many things since, but never the answers she had gone looking for. Now she looked back on it all as if it were a vivid dream with roots inexorably tangled in the waking world. A dream and a nightmare. All those years of wandering and desperate yearning, all those years of surviving.

Sometimes she missed those sudden and puzzling jaunts into other worlds, but not enough to cut herself loose of the anchor that now held her. For she was convinced it was their love that kept her here in the place she most wanted to be.

Grabbing a corner, she lifted the tarpaulin clear of the nearest mirror. This was the magic mirror, Miranda had explained, the one that went at the end of the show. Flat glass so it did not distort, simply offered a true reflection. But there was always something about it that drew Charlie, the call of the void, like a cliff edge might pull at someone who fears heights and falling.

The glass was like… black icy water into which her hand was disappearing. Absorbed as she was by the sensation in her fingers, the dryness once they were withdrawn, it wasn't until she stepped back that she became aware of the ash and cindered brick underfoot. She looked down wondering how it had got into the warehouse, how she had not noticed it before. Knew the warehouse was no longer there.

"No. Not now."

Her voice was soft, almost inaudible, lost in the endless tracts of destruction that surrounded her. Nothing stirred, not even the wind. She turned slowly on the spot and between her and the horizon there was nothing that was immediately familiar.

A blackened carcass of a tree rose from the ground nearby. Something about the configuration of the branches… She suddenly had trouble drawing breath as the landscape began to make sense. That small twisted tangle of metal, once a bike. That faint rectangle in the ashes, once a house. That shadow seared into a paving stone, once a person.

A person. Her hands began to tremble and a weakness at the knees made her stagger and turn. There had always been a way back before. Here she could not see it, could not sense it.

At first she thought it was her eyes playing tricks, a symptom of her growing panic. A shadow began to coalesce in the air. Faint, translucent, like a smudge of distant rainfall but close and getting closer without moving. It grew darker with more definite form until it burst in with the world and Miranda was whooping in a leap through the air, caught by Charlie and whirled around in astonished delight.

They stood in the silent warehouse, arms wrapped around each other, tears on Charlie's cheek. Miranda's embrace was fierce, making up for the months apart. Miranda's embrace was relentless.

"Like to breathe now," gasped Charlie.

"Daisy said you were here."

"But how… They said you were—"

"Beetle. She caught me crying like the soppy cow I am cos we parked up overnight. So she brought me home on her motorbike."

"What did Daisy say? Your Dad?"

Miranda shrugged. "Nothing. And I don't care if there is a row later."

She grabbed Charlie again and they spent a long time alone beside the mirrors in the dark.

The Old Wound Now Forgotten

You Can't Be True, Dear

The buzz of conversation filled the house, seeking out every corner and shady place, waxing and waning as it spread into the furthest places, seeping under cupboard doors, reaching up into the attic. Sometimes a muted laugh broke into the monotone, followed by a second of contemplative or appreciative silence before the contented hive-sound spread out again.

In the back hall near the kitchen and the door to what were once the servant's stairs it washed over a pocket of heavy silence that had formed around Charlie and Miranda. They stood frozen and watched as Daisy appeared from the kitchen carrying a tray piled high with sandwiches. She narrowed her eyes at them as she passed, her lips pressed tight. She looked frazzled. It was unseasonably warm and there were a lot of people back at the house that afternoon.

The volume of the buzz increased as Daisy pushed her way through the parlour door. As the door closed, Miranda returned to the attack.

"You were swinging it around like it was a trophy, something to be proud of."

Still stunned from the earlier onslaught, all Charlie could manage by way of a reply was: "I wasn't."

"Weren't you? How many autographs have you got on it?"

Charlie lifted her left arm and looked at the grubby cast on her wrist. It was covered with scrawled names and message. There was a beetle. A wall had been drawn and signed by Mary, Beth, and Lorna, a Kilroy peering over the top. Even Tom had put his name on it. She sagged a little when she saw his shaky signature. And despite what she'd said, it was true that she was a little bit proud of it. Like the bullet scar and all the other knocks and scrapes that had left their marks.

Before Charlie could say or do anything else, Daisy reappeared from the parlour, muted conversation following her out. She stopped in front of them, her face rough cut from stone.

"Are you two still bickering? It's been weeks now. And today of all days. Poor Tom fresh in his grave and you two… Show some respect. Get in there with the rest of the family and behave like adults or get out of the house and let us mourn in peace."

The minute Daisy was back in the kitchen, Miranda said: "And now you've got us into trouble with Daisy."

Charlie's heart was breaking and she didn't know what to do, had no defence against Miranda's cold anger, had never had to learn to defend herself against this sort of attack. Bombs, predators, police, bullies, no problem at all. Her best friend in all the world, the person she loved the most with a love that was a fierce burning star inside her and she had nothing.

Mute, she followed Miranda into the garden. Lost, bewildered, determined she was not going to cry even though she had not been nearer to tears than this since she saw her Nan's legs sticking out from the sheet down by the docks. Her head ached and tiny sparks of light kept flashing in her left eye.

Equally lost and unable to stop herself, Miranda continued as they came to a halt beneath the great oak tree.

"And I know for a fact you didn't break that when the tow bar fell on you like you said."

And that, too, was true. They had been out at Leatherhead practising on the bikes that Tom had been working on secretly for more than a year. She had broken it saving Lorna from a bad tumble when she had been trying a stunt she was told not to try until later when she was more accomplished. But Charlie wasn't going to let Lorna get into trouble so they'd staged the accident, the four of them. And kept it to themselves. Except Miranda somehow found out.

"Em… I. It's just that you worry so much."

"Of course I worry. I'm scared for all of you riding those bikes. You haven't even passed your tests yet and you're trying silly stunts. It's going to be even worse when you get that Wall together. I wish Tom had never bought it. How he kept it secret from the four of you I'll never know. I'll be worried sick. Every day. But that's your nature. You and the others. And it's your choice. I'm not going to stand in the way of it. I'll live with it. Mostly cos I know you're good at it and don't take risks like the others. It's not that I'm cross about." She drew in a deep breath. "You lied, Charlie. You lied to me. I wouldn't have told anyone what happened. You know that. But you didn't trust me. I had to overhear it."

"We didn't think—"

"We?"

"I didn't think it would be fair on you. If you'd known and Tom or Daisy or George had found out, then you'd have been put on the spot. Lie to them or rat us out."

It's what they'd decided but now, of course, it just sounded like a lame afterthought. After all, it was only a broken wrist. She could just as easily have done it tripping on the rough turf of the field at Leatherhead. She kicked herself. Why did the best solutions always come too late instead of all the subterfuge and unhappiness?

Miranda stalked off toward the house. Charlie wandered away to the warehouse and, in the darkness where Tom would never lurk again, she spent her seventeenth birthday crying.

A Little Bird Told Me

Twelfth Street Rag was blaring jauntily from the speakers, but it was late Wednesday evening and some of the sideshows were already closing up. George Russ was doing the rounds, talking to owners, checking the gaff lads all had somewhere decent to sleep. Daisy had gone back to their living van to make supper for the family.

"What's the time?" Miranda asked.

David looked at his watch. "Just shy of nine."

They looked at each other. "Up to you," said Miranda.

"Another ten minutes? Supper won't be ready for a while yet and we might get a last minute punter."

Miranda snorted and David kept his counsel. He didn't want another argument with his sister. There had been far too many in recent weeks. It didn't matter how careful any of them were, something always lit Miranda's touch paper. And there was never time to retire before the explosion.

They both looked out over the front of their parents stall. The usual hangers-on were still wandering about the ground, not taking the hint, dropping their chip wrappers everywhere, pushing each other about and generally not spending any money. It was one reason they closed up the fair in stages. It meant they were able to slowly increase the number of men on the watch for trouble, chancers who thought they could steal the takings or who were spoiling for a fight after they'd been drinking all evening.

Miranda wasn't worried. Not only was David's presence a reassurance, but she had learned to whistle and to call for help. There would be bodies there in seconds to protect them. David wasn't worried either. Even though he was slightly built and asthmatic, he knew anyone annoying Miranda would get a whole lot more than they asked for and serve them right.

"I'll start cleaning the rings."

David nodded and pulled out the bucket from under the prize table and placed it on the ground close to Miranda, the familiar odour of pine disinfectant overpowering the stale smell of fried onions. While Miranda squeezed out the cloth and began wiping the wooden rings, checking them for wear, he began dragging out the shutters from behind the stall.

When he didn't re-appear, Miranda looked round and saw Mary, Beth, and Lorna striding across the field toward the booth. She carried on wiping the rings. Not once did she take her eyes off the approaching group, noting that Lorna, as always, was just a few steps behind the other two.

It was Beth who stepped right up to the booth. "What have you said?"

"I've no idea what you're talking about, Bethany Tennant."

"Don't come Mrs Posh with me. You're not in your high chair any more."

"I've got work to do," said Miranda holding up a ring. "Unlike some, it seems."

"Charlie. What did you say to Charlie?"

"Nothing."

"That much is true," piped up David from a safe distance. "They haven't spoken in months."

Everyone turned to look at him and he wilted slowly under their gaze.

"Like I said," Miranda replied eventually. "Nothing."

"You must have. Why did you make her do it?"

Miranda shook her head, the hardness fading a fraction from her eyes. "What? What are you talking about? Nobody makes Charlie do anything she doesn't want."

"Not even you?"

"Especially me," she said ignoring the deputation and craning her neck to take in all the rides and sideshows, searching for the familiar figure. "What's happened? What's going on?"

Beth reached into a pocket of her overalls and pulled out a grubby envelope. Miranda dropped the ring and cloth from her hands and snatched the envelope from her, recognising Charlie's handwriting in the front. She pulled out the letter and read it. Then she read it again.

"Where is she?"

Everyone shrugged.

"Help David close up," she ordered.

No one dared argue; wouldn't have had time. Miranda vaulted the front of the booth and raced round to the living van.

Even in her anger she didn't dare cross the threshold with dirty footwear, so stood at the top of the steps as her mother turned from the stove.

"Have you seen Charlie?"

Daisy glanced at the clock. "Surely she's normally at the rifles this time of night. Anyway I thought you two weren't talking."

"Mum?"

Daisy was startled. She hadn't heard Miranda use that word for a long time. "Are you all right, my love? Maybe your father will know."

But she was speaking to an open doorway and the clatter of boots down the outside steps.

Miranda tracked down her father by the bumper cars. He saw her coming and broke off his conversation with the owner of the ride to meet her part way. Something about the way she strode across the soggy ground.

"Have you seen Charlie?" Breathless. Angry.

"She's not here, love."

"What?"

The main lights on the bumper cars went out leaving them in darkness. There was laughter as shutters were dropped into place with a crash and locked.

"She went with Jack and Dan out to Bicester. There was an auction today. Some decent lorries. Generators."

"When are they back?"

"No idea. If they bought anything they'll drive it down to Leatherhead."

Miranda was off again, across the field to where the girls had their living van. She didn't knock.

"Oi!" said Lorna as the opened door caught her half-dressed at the stove.

Miranda edged past to Charlie's bunk. It was neatly made. Her cupboard was completely empty. Her bag gone. Nothing of her remained.

The other three watched her nervously as she turned, face tight with anger, tears in her eyes.

"I didn't..."

She couldn't manage any more and ran out of the van.

At three in the morning she was woken by the familiar purr of Charlie's Blue Star as it came onto the field and sputtered to a stop. After a moment's silence in which she struggled free of dark dreams, she heard the whistled opening bars of 'My Buddy', a song from the '20s they all used to identify themselves as a member of the fair to whoever was on night watch.

Already dressed, she snuck out of the family van and into the cool night. Charlie was pushing her bike across the grass to her own van. Miranda followed, barefooted on the damp grass.

Charlie jumped when she felt her ear grabbed, offered up no resistance as a fierce Miranda dragged her past the vans and through a gap in the hedge to the adjacent field.

"What…? Oh. I'm too angry."

Charlie stood, head bowed, trying to remain attached to her ear. Miranda looked at her hand, realising she was squeezing hard. She let go.

"Why did you write that letter? I thought you'd gone for good."

"Didn't George explain?"

"Your stuff was gone."

"I might have had to stay at Leatherhead. As it was, there was time to get back here."

"Why? Why did you want to come back? Why did you write that letter? You can't give up the Wall."

There was a moment's silence in the dark. Charlie rubbed at her left eye, annoyed by the little flecks of light that had sparked and gone. "Can if I want."

"But why would you. That's stupid. It's all you four ever wanted to do."

They had been hissing in the dark night. Now there was silence as Charlie moved her hand to her ear and rubbed that, staring at the vague outline of Miranda radiating anger.

"I'm given it up because it's making you miserable and because I lost you and I don't want you afraid and I want you back. I hate all this anger and not talking and—"

She didn't finish because Miranda had leapt at her in the dark, pounding at her with small fists. Charlie staggered back. The onslaught was fierce and painful. The only way she could think to stop it was to step into it and wrap her arms around Miranda, pulling her in close.

Charlie waited until she felt Miranda relax, and then loosened her grip a little.

"I thought you'd gone," said Miranda, her voice small in the dark

"And leave you?"

She couldn't say any more because Miranda was kissing her and crying and shaking.

Charlie waited, her arms still round Miranda not caring if anyone saw. When she had her mouth back, she said: "There's lots I can do. It doesn't have to be the Wall."

"Don't be silly. You must do the Wall. You can't not do it now."

Charlie sighed.

"You two all right?" whispered Beth from the other side of the hedge.

"We're fine, Beetle," said Charlie. "And tear up that letter."

"God, you two. Sort yourselves out. It's getting on my nerves."

They heard Beth stumbling away in the dark and kissed again. Soft at first and then passionate and then hands exploring and then… all the old frustrations because it was secret and they were never properly alone and even if they were…

Far Away Places

Rain swept up the length of Queen's Road to greet them as they left the station.

"We won't be seeing much of Brighton if it stays like this," said Miranda. She huddled deeper into her pea jacket as Charlie buttoned her greatcoat.

Charlie nudged her. "I thought that was the idea."

"Stop it. Now are we going to stand here in the rain all day or are we going to find Mrs Barber's Guest House?"

"Lead the way, then. Your relative."

The piece of paper that Miranda pulled out her pocket flapped in the wind. They each held a corner and looked at the crudely drawn map. Straight ahead. First left. Down the hill. First right and not too far past the corner shop.

Leaning into the wind, their rucksacks on their backs, they made their way down the road, turned left, trotted down the slope and then turned right, passing the small general store. They were faced with a long, narrow street lined with terraced houses and workshops. The houses immediately beyond the corner shop were larger and double-fronted. Number 5, Mrs Barber's Guest House, was one of them. Beyond, the houses were smaller, the terrace broken by several broad alleys that lead to courtyards and workshops at the rear. They stood in the rain and Miranda lifted the heavy brass knocker and rapped twice.

The door opened and they were greeted by an effusive midget of a woman.

"In. In. Come on in. You must be soaked. Frozen. Get those things off and I'll hang them by the range in the kitchen. Soon have them dry. I'm Caroline. Mum had pretensions, see, but everyone calls me Carrie, so you do just that. How was your journey? It was such a surprise to hear from Daisy. And I was so sorry to hear about Tom. And you two needing a holiday. You don't look old enough to be worn out yet. Bless you both. Come on in. Don't worry about them boots."

Concussed by the welcome, they followed Mrs Barber along a hallway and into a large kitchen.

"I put you two in the big room up front. Hope that's all right. Anyway you'll see for yourself. Get set by that range and I'll brew some tea. Put your bags anywhere. That's right. Stretch out. My you've got long legs. Charlotte is it? And Miranda. Look at you. Quite the young lady now. And so beautiful."

Miranda went the colour of beetroot as Charlie winked at her with a broad grin behind Mrs Barber's back.

"Both of you. Look at you. You'll have to be fighting the lads off, no doubt. Listen to me. Anyway, no two ways about it. Time for all the news and gossip."

Surprisingly she let them talk. Most of it came from Miranda as she knew the family in a way Charlie never would.

They were plied with more tea and sandwiches and cake until eventually Mrs Barber saw how tired they both were.

"What am I thinking, keeping you here? You must be tired after your journey and me gabbing on like I always do. Let's get you up to your room. It's the one in the front. Or did I already tell you that? You won't mind sharing will you?"

The landing was lit from above by a skylight and the door Mrs Barber opened revealed a bright room with twin beds.

"It's just right," said Charlie. "Much more room than we're used to on the road."

"That'll be so. And Mr B has just painted it. White is all we could get, cover up that dull old wallpaper. A bit stark I thought, but nice and bright when it's gloomy like it has been. Shame about them curtains, but that blackout material's got a lot of wear in it yet. Oh. And here's a front door key. I don't usually, but as you're family… Anyway, I'll let you sort yourselves out. Bathroom's just there. Breakfast at eight."

Mrs Barber bustled out and Charlie closed the door, softly turning the key. Miranda collapsed on one of the beds, a pillow over her face, convulsed with silenced laughter.

Together

The sun was shining when Miranda woke. The bed was warm, Charlie's right arm held her close; she could feel the naked body beside her.

"Heaven," she whispered.

Charlie did not move. Miranda turned her head to see if she was still asleep. It had been a tiring week. But Charlie was not sleeping. She lay, head cradled in her left arm, staring at the ceiling.

"Are you all right? You look like you've seen a… Oh."

"No. Not yet."

"What? What do you mean, 'not yet'?"

"I…"

Charlie turned her head slowly again, but the echoes of things yet to be had faded along with the pale rainbow bars of light that had taken to plaguing her left eye and the room was just a bedroom in a Brighton boarding house.

Miranda propped herself up on one elbow. "Charlie?"

Charlie sighed and made herself smile. "Do you remember, years ago, when I was ill? Daisy had to get the doctor?"

Miranda leaned across Charlie and kissed the scar on Charlie's left arm. "That's what I suddenly thought of," she said after she'd brushed Charlie's lips with her own.

"You asked me if they were ghosts," said Charlie wanting nothing more than to make love with Miranda again but knowing she had to go on with the conversation.

"Were they?"

"No. I… I don't know."

"And those things you told me in the warehouse about your life. It's all a bit dreamlike now."

"I wish that's all it…"

"Charlie?"

"I'm scared."

"Of ghosts?"

"No. Yes. No. Not that."

Miranda shook her head, sought under the sheet for Charlie's hand and held it tight. "What then?"

"No lies. Nothing hidden."

"I don't understand."

"I'm scared that if I tell you everything you won't believe me."

"Why wouldn't I?"

"Because sometimes I don't believe it myself."

Miranda gathered Charlie close. In the white room with black curtains Charlie told her everything, her whole life from her earliest memories of sitting in the dust watching the sparrows with lake and mountains in the background, her mother singing on the veranda right through to the present day, things lost and gained, all the strange adventures along the way, the ghost children, the people who had visited her, the strange worlds… Everything except that one, icy nightmare she had vowed to keep to herself.

It was quiet for a long time after she had finished. The light was fading. Miranda lay close cuddled against Charlie's side. Charlie was beginning to think she had drifted off to sleep when she stirred.

"Next time."

"Yes?"

"Take me as well."

The shadows in Charlie's mind faded before an inner dawn light and she closed her eyes, contented, queen of the world.

Riders In The Sky

"You spelled that wrong."

"What?"

Charlie stepped back, paintbrush in hand, to look at her handiwork.

"Ha. Had you going there for a moment."

"Get lost, Beetle!"

Everyone else stood sniggering.

The smell of paint filled the old hangar even though the doors were wide open to let in the weak January sunshine. Charlie had been hard at work all morning, keeping her mind occupied. The others had been helping until recently when Miranda had arrived with a tray of tin mugs filled with tea that steamed in the cool air.

They were all waiting for the meeting to finish. Charlie could have attended. She owned a share. But she didn't think it right until she was twenty-one and running a ride of her own. And she knew there were other owners who felt the same.

Sipping her tea, she surveyed their handiwork, blinking away the tiny spark of light from her left eye. All the parts of the Wall were propped up in sequence round the inside of the hangar. They had spent all winter camped outside in a caravan so they could assess the state of the ride, get some of the older men to do a bit of welding, and then laboriously rub down all the metalwork and coat it with red oxide primer.

Whilst they'd been doing that they had discussed what colour the top coat should be and whether they'd be able to get enough paint in that colour, whether the bikes should match, and how they could possibly afford a professionally painted sign. Charlie had also suggested names for the bikes and the act which met with their approval.

She had shrugged at their praise. "Seemed sensible to me. The bikes are Indians. And we're all princesses." There had been sniggering at that as well. So the Indian Princesses it was.

“Have you made your minds up yet?” asked Charlie.

Beth, Mary, and Lorna were still looking at the list Charlie had given them, written in Miranda’s neat hand.

“Where’d you get these names anyway? Are they real?” Mary asked.

“Course they are,” chipped in Miranda. “We went to see Fred, Alice’s son.”

The girls looked blank.

“He retired ages ago,” said Miranda, “but he worked a Wild West show for years. Got loads of books on it. They’re all real women Indian Chiefs and Warriors. Pictures as well. Lovely clothes.”

“Not much good for riding the Wall, though,” said Charlie.

“Well we reckon,” said Mary, “that you should have first choice—”

“Pine Leaf.”

“—because you did the work finding them.”

They looked at Charlie who grinned. Miranda smiled a private smile as well.

“And we’ll put the other names in a hat.”

Miranda took off her woolly hat and threw it to Beth who held it open as Mary tore up the list with care.

“Lorna first.”

“I’m just the back-up.”

They all blew raspberries.

“You always say that. You’re part of the team. No escape now.”

Lorna grinned and put her hand in the upturned hat.

“Morning Glory. I like that.”

Mary nudged her out of the way and pushed her hand into the hat. “Willow Walker.”

“The real name is ‘In Amongst The Willows’ but I didn’t think I’d get that on the bike’s tank,” said Charlie.

“It’s good. Like it. All willowy just like me.”

More raspberries were blown, although fair to say Mary was almost as tall as Charlie who was turning into a regular bean-pole, though no one ever dared called her that.

"Go on, Beth," said Miranda.

"Ooh. Running Eagle."

She handed the hat back to Miranda who pulled it over her head, winking at Charlie from behind the others' backs.

And then there was the Wall itself. When they'd been cleaning it, they found one of the upright panels had a faint chalk inscription, presumably put there by the seller to mark who the new owner was. 'Old Tom', it said. And that's how they had started referring to the Wall. And now Charlie had made it official, painting it in ornate letters on the panel that fitted over the entrance to the interior.

"He'd like that."

They all turned from their contemplation of Charlie's painting to see George and Daisy standing together in the open doorway.

There was an awkward silence. Daisy, who had made the comment, nudged George.

"Yes. The meeting. First thing, before I forget. Harry reported he'd been... 'approached' by a shady type. Wanted to know if the fair might be interested in moving a few boxes when it goes on the road. Harry told them 'No'. Politely. Made up some bunkum about police checking fairs on a regular basis. We've let the Guild know and we're telling you in case you get approached. It's bad enough we get spivs on the fairground flogging stuff out of suitcases, but this is something new. First hint of anything dodgy, straight to me or Daisy, please."

They all nodded.

George cleared his throat.

"The Wall." He waved his hand to where Charlie had been painting. "'Old Tom'. Some concerns raised. Tom paid a lot out for it. It's not earning. Some wanted it sold."

"That's not fair. Everyone knows we can't run it till we're twenty-one," said Mary.

Beth stood beside her, frowning.

"Which is why," said Daisy, "we came up with a solution."

"The Wall belongs to Simmons Fair," said George. "Tom made sure of that. All properly legal. Like Alice's Gallopers.

And a lot of the penny machines. Not sure how he came up with the idea, but everyone agreed."

Charlie smiled to herself, remembering that small, untidy figure when she had first seen him, his cardigan unravelling; recalling the stormy night when she'd made the suggestion. A shiver crawled across her flesh as she recalled the other even of that day.

"It means the fair as a whole now has an income to cover emergencies. So it wants the Wall up and running."

"What?" Beth sounded startled. "When?"

"If you can prove to me by the end of the year that you can do a show safely, it goes on the road start of season 1950. You've got a year."

"But we haven't got an act," said Charlie. "Or a lorry. Or anything to transport the bikes."

"Well," said Daisy with an impish smile. "You'd better get a move on, then. You won't sort it out by standing there looking glum or gawping at George. And if you make a go of it, you'll be made joint owners when the last of you is twenty-one. After that you can sort out the arrangements yourselves."

With a wink, she took George's arm and the pair of them went back out into the winter sunshine.

The Princesses stood staring at one another with nervous grins. Turning, Charlie saw the brave smile on Miranda's face.

"Right," she said. "We need to draw up a timetable. First thing is to finish painting 'Old Tom'. Then we need to practice on our bikes. On the flat first cos we can do that while we're on the road. Then we need to find a living van and something to transport the bikes. We could convert a coach or something. Then we need two lorries."

"Two?" asked Lorna.

"Yes. Cos Em's helped us all this time without ever needing to be asked so, as well as getting the Wall ready to go, we're going to build her a show so she can take her mirrors on the road."

Slipping Around

Perched on the roof of the House of Fun, tucked in behind the painted display, Charlie had an unbroken view of the whole fair. She ignored it. Despite the noise and lights and the wailing from the ghost train, despite the mingled smells of candyfloss and frying onions, despite the laughter and shouts, she had a book.

Nobody had said she couldn't have a book up there even though she was meant to be keeping watch. They'd had a spate of trouble, spivs selling things, drunks causing trouble, more pressure from black marketeers. Life was hard enough on the road without the extra problems these people brought.

She could read the fairground now as easily as she could the book in her hand. A quick glance every time she turned a page was enough to know that it was a normal Friday evening, that it was early and mostly families filling the spaces between the rides and the stalls, wandering aimlessly and enjoying a bit of brightness and loud music, watching other people do the same.

Happy there was no trouble, her eyes flicked back down to the library book spread on her lap. It was uncomfortable reading. She had experienced this world first hand, and not just because of the deprivations of the blitz. She had stepped into it. More than once. And she did not understand how that could be. Had the author also travelled? Had he stood in the ruins of all those other Londons perpetually at war?

She felt especially engaged as at the heart of the book was a love story that society held to be illicit. She did not feel her love for Miranda was wrong. Of that she was fiercely adamant. But the rest of the world?

At the end of the chapter, she marked her place with a ticket and closed the book, sliding it into the deep inner pocket of her Guthrie. With the bleak Orwellian nightmare still in her head she looked back down at the wild delights of the fairground for some respite.

To start with she looked straight to the Russ stall and her eyes found Miranda and could not help but linger. A little taste of honey. With a smile and a sigh of contentment she dragged her gaze away and surveyed the rest of the crowd. It was beginning to get dark now and the fading sky disappeared beyond the pool of light and sound beneath her.

Although the crowds always seemed chaotic, especially at ground level, and were never quite the same in temperament from one day to the next, they did follow patterns. Early in the week, they were quieter, thinner, slower. By Thursday they were getting fuller. Friday and Saturday were the big money nights. They were also the most troublesome. Saturday especially. They stayed open late. It was pay day for a lot of people, especially youths who moved from the pubs to the fair. The penny machines were locked away and everyone manned the rides and sideshows, with floaters like Charlie keeping an eye open from above and directing squads to quell trouble before it got out of hand.

Most times it was just a bit of shouting, usually round the rifle range, accusations of bent barrels. Charlie knew none of the guns had been tampered with. She shot most days and could hit any target they put up for her with any rifle. It was the drink that made the toughs inaccurate; it was the drink that then made them belligerent.

Below, the crowds continued to circulate. They were there for fun and moved from sideshow to sideshow, ride to ride, stopped in groups to talk and laugh over candyfloss, or eat a hotdog, suck up a fizzy drink from a bottle. Which made it all the easier to see those who didn't conform, who weren't there for the fun but for their own ends.

Usually it was someone standing still for a long time in an out of the way place. Not someone waiting for a friend; they would stand by the entrance or in the bright lights of a ride. It was those who kept to the shadows you watched. Those and the ones who moved counter to the crowd. The ones who didn't go from ride to ride, but who followed others, looking for unguarded wallets and purses, passing off to an accomplice. The ones who came with a suitcase looking for some shadowy gap where they could try and sell nylons or cigarettes or whatever else had fallen their way from the back of a lorry. Charlie knew them all.

One she didn't know she was watching now. Rather, she was watching the way the crowds moved around a shadowy figure that somehow kept just out of sight. Almost as if he had seen someone on a high perch keeping watch. Charlie eased herself back into shadow and moved along the roof of the Fun House behind the wooden banner. Half way along was a small hole. She peered through, found who she was looking for and sat back, heart thumping, an extremely rude work escaping her lips.

Instinctively, she followed it with a "Sorry, Nan."

It was a reflex that hadn't kicked in for a long time, but the sight of Sideways Billy below jerked her back to her childhood.

Scrambling forward, she pressed her eye to the hole again. Sure enough he was still there, scuttling sideways on his crippled legs. He came to a stop beside someone who was also keeping to shadow. Charlie moved to the far end of the Fun House roof to get a better look. Her heart sank further. Ronnie Ollis.

With the bitter taste of bile in her throat, she climbed down the back of the Fun House and went looking for Harry. There had been a brief moment of relief that Ollis had survived the wild beating she had given him. But her stomach curdled at the memory of all the miseries he and his gang had inflicted on her.

Stepping onto the gallopers at full speed was something she had learned early on and she encouraged the other Princesses to do it as often as possible. It helped train the mind and body to work with odd forces acting on them. Beth was there collecting money. She waved and Charlie waved back as she made her way to the centre between the rising and falling horses, the flailing hands and feet of the riders.

At the centre, Harry saw her swing past several times. It was pointless trying to talk above the sound of the music blasting away. As Charlie passed again he pointed to his chest with his thumb and she nodded.

On Charlie's next pass he stepped up onto the deck and they both made their way to the edge, Harry signalling to Beth to take over.

Back on the grass, Harry found someone to help Beth and then faced Charlie.

"You look like you've seen a ghost, girl," he said.

She watched his lips. They were still close to the gallopers and she could only half hear his words.

"I think I might have."

A querulous frown crossed Harry's face. Charlie beckoned and he followed.

They made their way round the back of the gallopers and through the living vans to emerge by the Ghost Train.

"Over by the rifles," said Charlie in Harry's ear. "Is that the one who approached you at the beginning of the year?"

"What? Those two over there?"

Charlie nodded.

"Nah," said Harry. "For one thing he was a good bit older. Same type though. Oily. You know them?"

Charlie sighed. "A long time ago. Tall one is Ronnie Ollis. The other one I only ever knew as Sideways Billy. There used to be five of them. Ollis was the worst. A real bad 'un. Nick-your-stuff-while-you're-sleeping-in-an-air-raid-shelter bad."

"And pick on girls?"

Charlie nodded.

"I'll pass the word," said Harry and was gone.

Within minutes he would have passed on descriptions of Ollis and Billy to all the owners. One or two of them sauntered by to have a look for themselves, winking at Charlie as they passed.

Much to her surprise, Ollis was joined by a young woman. Charlie didn't know who she was but immediately felt sorry for her. Whatever had drawn her into Ronnie Ollis's orbit can't have been good; any more than staying there would end well.

Old angers seethed in her depths. When Ollis and his companion moved off, with Billy trailing behind as they moved from sideshow to sideshow, Charlie shadowed them replaying all the grim memories, right up to that last encounter.

"Cor. It's ther little barsterd," Ollis had said. "We eard you was dead."

"Praps I'm a ghost, then," she'd replied.

"Ain't scared of you."

That's when she'd beaten him to a pulp in a volcanic explosion of fury, leaving him unconscious on a pavement as the others ran. Never knowing until now whether he'd survived. And she still hated him.

When Ollis and his friends queued up for the Ghost Train it was too good an opportunity to miss. Charlie got the nod from Herbert Cutwood and slipped round the back. All fairgrounds are façade. Behind the gaudily painted and brightly lit frontages, the workings were plain to see. Only the gallopers sustained the illusion all the way round.

The back of the Ghost Train was plain black board, with a door for access to maintain and clean the track. Charlie listened for a car to rumble by and then slipped inside. Using her torch, she stepped across the convoluted windings of the track, ducked under one of the 'frights' and made her way to a small alcove behind the façade where a chink in the boards allowed her to see out.

Ollis and his companion were climbing into one of the cars Charlie had long ago helped to restore. The young woman looked excited. Ollis was trying to look tough. They jerked as the car started forward and Charlie stepped over the rail, heading for the spot she wanted close by the exit. She switched off her torch.

The car clattered through the entrance doors and into the dark. Sirens went off, a crone cackled, lights flashed, the car jerked round corners drawing closer. Skeletons danced, giant spiders bounced, monsters lurched, and by the exit, in a lurid green light, Charlie leaned out, wailing like a spirit in torment.

Ronnie Ollis was out of the car before it cleared the exit doors, leaving Sideways Billy to help the young woman out of the car when it came to a stop. Confused, they watched as a frightened Ollis pushed his way through the crowds, eventually following. And Charlie watched them with grim satisfaction. It had been childish, but she went on her way to the Russ stall, light of heart.

Fair White Wings

Bewitched

They had done it so often it filled their dreams. All through the previous twelve months, between each set up and pull down, they had crammed themselves into an Austin 7 Ruby that had seen far better days and driven down to Leatherhead. Breakdowns were frequent to begin with, but they always managed to patch the old machine back together. By year's end they had virtually rebuilt it and made the journey without incident.

Once in Leatherhead they spent all their time on the Wall, converting the coach and lorry, painting, practising setting up and pulling down and, when they felt confident, venturing onto the boards on their Indian bikes. The day they all went horizontal for the first time was exhilarating.

They also visited other fairs where Walls were attractions and watched shows, talking about what they had seen and constructing a programme of their own.

And when Simmons pulled down for the last time in 1949 and the field and sheds at Leatherhead filled up with trucks and rides in need of maintenance, they put on shows for their fellows.

Now it was Tuesday 14 February 1950. First show of the year. Out front, Lorna was riding her bike on the rollers and Harry was on the microphone putting out a line of patter over the speakers. Inside, the Princesses, decked out in buckskin leggings and shirts, knee length moccasins, their hair in plaits, waited nervously, checking their bikes one last time as people appeared on the gallery at the top of the Wall.

They knew their act inside out. They were all nervous.

The door opened and Harry climbed into the interior, followed by Miranda.

Charlie frowned. "What are you doing in here?"

Miranda poked the tip of her tongue out and from behind her back produced four silk red rosebuds.

"Couldn't very well give one just to you without eyebrows being raised," she whispered as she attached it to Charlie's shirt front. "But this one is specially for my Valentine."

With a wink she passed on to the others then came back to Charlie as Harry announced the show and the engines roared.

"Stay safe," she said and made her way out through the door. Harry checked it was properly closed and retreated to the centre as the bikes roared into life.

And then, for Charlie, there was just the narrow wooden road ahead of her, the world turning like a wheel out of the corner of each eye. To her right the thin line of spectators turned counter clockwise, to her left the centre of the arena turned clockwise. She wove up and down the Wall and then dropped down the angle to the floor whilst Beth and Mary took their turns.

For quarter of an hour they performed their roster of stunts and then, drenched with sweat despite the cold weather, they sat grinning at one another as the gallery above emptied and Harry slipped outside to begin his spiel all over again. Miranda came back in with a jug of coffee and mugs and poured them each a drink which they gulped greedily, still grinning, their heads still filled with the roar of the bikes and the whirl of the world they had just conquered.

Count Every Star

Charlie paused as she crossed the field to stare up into the night sky. It was a rare moment alone, a rare moment away from the roar and thunder of the Wall, from music blaring out of the speakers, from grease and dirt and exhaust fumes. From other people.

She shook her head. All those years she had hidden away as the bombs fell. Now she was part of big, boisterous, sometimes bad tempered, but mostly loving family that worked all hours in their nomadic life, with mud their worst enemy.

For the longest moment she did not know, could not be sure, was unable to separate her sense of tiredness from the possibility that the faint loop of light arching in the dark in front of her was real.

The dissociation with reality was further compounded by the nature of what she saw. On the very edge of vision to begin with, defying her attempts to focus on the faint wisp of light, it resembled nothing less than the corona of the sun, something she had seen in a Pathé newsreel years earlier.

Unable to focus, she could not determine whether the icy, sapphire blue was a great distance away or right in front of her, perhaps within her, like the sparks of light had been during the last few years.

Was it real? Was she dreaming? Going mad?

She knew it couldn't be the northern lights. She'd read about those. Curtains of light in the sky, mostly green. What she saw was right in front of her, the blue of glaciers growing slowly denser, a slow motion fountain, several plumes erupting from some point near the muddy ground and arcing up and out, twisting and flaring as they curved.

And as she watched, transfixed, it evolved. The colour grew stronger, the turning columns of light grew less chaotic, weaving themselves into a multi-stranded column that rotated on its vertical axis. Like a drunken dancer it leaned in one direction, moving off that way before it corrected itself, teetered, and then headed off in another direction, all the while staying in the same place, vast and tiny, filling the universe, leaving the field dark and filling her head with fierce, writhing strings of light.

Time ceased to have any meaning as the eruption became, without any discernible change, like a giant lotus flower. It turned for an eternity before the petals began to close, forming a bright, ovoid, many-faceted jewel, turning in the dark in front of her.

At the same time, she knew it for something she had once glimpsed in the past. Or possibly the future. It was a lighthouse, a threshold, a doorway, an opening to the worlds she had long since given up hope of ever visiting again, happy that what anchored her was far more important. And yet, there, in front of her, a breath of exotic air teasing her senses, the eerie touch of static against her flesh, the scent of roses and sandalwood, sudden and inexplicable on the night air.

A memory flashed into her mind of her mother's panic, just before the long journey out of Kashmir, away from the dazzling waters of Dal to the grimy streets of Deptford; that frantic search through the small bungalow for the missing sapphire. She reached a hand toward the lotus of light, drawn to its promise… and let the hand drop.

Had Miranda been there with her, she would have led her through and they would have stood side by side in some other world, even if for a moment. But Miranda was not there. She turned her back on it, noting that bright as the light was she cast no shadow on the grass, and blinked back the tears as she strode away.

Rust Upon Iron

Domino

Head to one side on the pillow, Charlie watched the doors at the far end of the room, struggling to keep her eyes open.

"You expecting anyone, dear?"

Charlie turned her head a little more and the woman in the next bed came into view, slightly out of focus. She nodded. Slowly. Nausea made her stop.

"I've got no one in till this evening, so if there's more than two, they can pretend to sit with me. I won't mind."

"Thanks." It came out as a quiet croak through parched lips.

The woman winked and went back to her knitting.

Charlie turned her head back to face the double doors again. Somewhere beyond them there was a loud metallic clatter and Charlie winced.

"Just a trolley, dear," came the soothing voice above the gentle click of needles.

Charlie watched as the Ward Sister pushed one of the doors open and peered into the corridor. Her face was stony when she came back in and returned to her table in the centre of the room. When she sat, she disappeared behind the large vase of flowers.

It was whispering that woke Charlie again. When her eyes opened they were still fixed on the door. Long groggy moments passed before she realised the ward was full; moments more before the figure beside her bed came into focus.

"Em."

Before Miranda could reply, other voices broke in from behind her.

"Is she awake now?" asked Beth.

Miranda nodded and Charlie, even through the after effects of the sedatives, could see she was angry and scared and relieved, wanted to hold her and reassure her and cursed that she didn't even dare hold her hand.

She hoped it was in her eyes, that Miranda could read it there.

Before she had a chance to find out, Mary and Beth scuttled into view, watching out for the nurses.

"Shove over for a sec, Em. We've got to get away soon. Show opens at six."

"What's the…" It seemed to take her forever.

"Never mind that. Important stuff. Your bike is all right. Bit dented but nothing major and we'll have it fixed before you're mended. Old Tom is fine. A few splinters."

"Never mind the bikes," objected Miranda. "The important thing is you're all right."

"Apart from all those broken bones," chipped in Mary with a grin over Beth's shoulder.

Mary reached out an arm and dragged Lorna into view. Lorna gave a little wave. Charlie smiled dreamily. "Three of you. Be careful."

"Two visitors only to a bed," interrupted a stern voice. "Can't have people littering the place up."

"Sorry miss," said Beth over her shoulder after flickering a wink in Charlie's direction. "We've got to go now anyway. See you later Charlie."

Mary and Lorna also said their goodbyes and the three of them chattered off down the length of the ward, their good natured voices drowning the quiet murmur of other visitors.

The Ward Sister looked sternly at Miranda for a moment, back straight, hands held across the front of her dark blue uniform. With a nod she turned and walked away.

"She barks," said the woman in the next bed, "but she don't bite. You sit over the other side, dear, more private for you."

Miranda said a quiet thank you and after straightening the chairs went round to the other side of Charlie's bed. Charlie turned slowly, one leg anchored in place by the weight of the plaster encasing it. By the time she was settled again all the anger had gone from Miranda's face, replaced by tears.

"Here," said Charlie quietly, moving her right arm on the cover. "Hold my hand. No one will see."

Miranda couldn't speak for a long time, simply held tight to Charlie's bandaged hand. After a while, she realised she was gripping it too hard and let go.

"It's all right," lied Charlie. "Doesn't hurt. Just a little scrape on that one."

Miranda knew it was a lie; she'd been there when they disentangled Charlie from the bike and had ridden with her in the back of the ambulance.

"What happened?" Miranda managed to ask.

"I don't know. We hadn't even got to the tricky stuff. I was up near the top of the Wall and then I wasn't. I'm sorry, Em."

"You didn't do it on purpose, did you. So don't be sorry. Just be thankful it's only bones."

Charlie lifted her hand and Miranda took hold again, gently this time.

"I love you," Charlie mouthed silently.

Miranda blushed. "Ssh," she said as she squeezed just a little tighter. "I'll have to go soon. Catch the bus. George and Daisy will be in this evening. Harry's barking for the show and John and me will be running the hoopla stall. I've put a bag of your things in your bedside locker. Flannel, soap, clean underwear, fresh nightie. There's some pads as well. I know you're not due on yet, but who knows what a fall will do. And all those drugs."

"Is there a mirror?"

Miranda nodded.

"Don't be frightened by what you see. Your face. Your lovely face. Charlie." The tears came back for a moment, scrubbed away. "And there's your book and some of those magazines, back copies of *Fantax*, a new *Meteor*, and a couple of *Les Pionniers*. And your French dictionary."

"Em," said Charlie to stop the panicked flow.

"What?"

Charlie stuck out the tip of her tongue.

"It's all right for you," said Miranda, cross again. "I was worried sick. Don't you ever do it again."

There was nothing Charlie could say, but it didn't matter because Miranda poked out the tip of her tongue and the world was all right.

It's All In The Game

Charlie had managed some bread and butter and a cup of tea and been wheelchaired to the bathroom before Daisy and George arrived. She was sitting propped against a pile of pillows when they appeared. Daisy brought flowers; George wielded a tin of sweets. And there was a get well card crammed with signatures. Charlie cried. Daisy enveloped her in a feather light embrace. George fussed ineffectually.

Eventually, after conferences with the Ward Sister, they were reassured that Charlie was in no danger, simply needed time to let the broken bones knit and the bruises fade.

"Will you please impress that on Em?" she asked. "She looked so worried when she left earlier. Just let her know I am all right."

They all had a laugh at that as they surveyed the bandages and heavy leg cast, the bruising and grazes covered with iodine. None of them laughed for long. And when visiting time was over, they both hugged Charlie and she got tearful again, was asleep within minutes of the doors closing behind them.

And So To Sleep Again

Tiny echoes and distant footsteps growing and fading. The rustling of papers, blown in a lazy warm breeze. A flicker of electric blue. A sure knowledge that the corridors went on forever, that all the doors were locked, and that at every turn, as if someone had just passed, there lingered the hint of sandalwood and rose.

Tiredness drenched her, soaked her bones, dragged her down. She floated and sank, drifted up again, became aware of a cooling hand on her brow and a smiling face, before slipping away into darkness once more.

Out on the long walkways, climbing the ladders in dark interiors with the wind thrumming against the outer skin, standing now and then to watch the lights blinking on the distant towers before moving on, hiding, running, wheeling, riding with the world rotating on either side, the staring faces, a gentle smile always just out of reach.

The quiet step of the nurse moving from bed to bed in the light from the lamp on the table in the middle of the ward. A thin, pale face appearing in one of the porthole windows of the double doors. Drifting in the warmth of her bed, conscious of every ache, pain, itch, and burn, gasping a little as she moved to find a more comfortable position.

Sparrow In The Treetop

Breakfast came and went, blanket baths for the bed bound, the dispensing of pills and taking of temperatures, cleaning and sweeping, all under the watchful eye of the Ward Sister.

Whilst doctors were doing their rounds, the woman in the bed next to Charlie said: "I thought them what came to see you yesterday evening was your parents."

Charlie was about to explain but replied: "They are." Not because she didn't want to explain, but because it was true.

"Oh. Sorry. That'll teach me to be nosy. Just the likeness."

Charlie frowned.

"You. And that woman they let in during the night. Thought *she* must be your Mum."

Charlie's heart skipped a beat. She wanted to know more but the doctor arrived and the curtains were pulled. By the time they were drawn back, the woman in the next bed had gone.

Out In The Cold Again

Even though she'd only been there a day and a half, events began to blur and she lost all sense of time. She read a lot, ate the food that was put in front of her, did as she was told by the nurses, and went back to reading.

Afterwards, when the nurse had cleaned her up and changed the sheets, she wondered just how she had managed to read so far into the magazine article without realizing. The headline 'Unsolved Crimes of the Blackout' should have given it away. Perhaps it was the drugs they had given her, the shock of the fall. But she kept reading, of petty theft and counterfeiters, of black market scams, drawn deeper into the darkness until she was living the nightmare on the page in front of her. The story of how young girls had been abducted and murdered, with hints of worse between, of the beast never apprehended. The throwing aside of the magazine and vomiting all down her front.

The nurses put it down to delayed reaction to the crash and fussed over her for a while, but the banished memories had returned.

(It's No) Sin

And then Miranda was there and the world was brighter and the time soared by. It felt like they'd hardly had time to say hello before the visiting hours' bell rang and chairs scraped and hands were squeezed and Charlie tried to distract herself by sorting through the books and magazines that Miranda had left.

She was sniffing back a tear when the woman in the next bed said: "Well, that's me."

Charlie turned slowly, her neck stiffer than it had been.

Her neighbour was up and dressed, another woman standing beside her holding a bag.

"Oh. Going home? Well. Goodbye."

Charlie wanted to ask about her night time visitor, but knew it would sound odd. She watched as the two women turned and headed for the door, her neighbour walking slowly and leaning on the arm of her companion. After a few steps they stopped. There was a quick whispered conversation and her neighbour slowly returned, right up to her bedside.

"None of my business," she said, talking so quietly Charlie could barely hear. "Too nosy for my own good Amy says." She nodded toward her companion. "Probably right. Anyway. And if I've got it wrong. But..." She took a deep breath. "You and your friend who's just gone."

Charlie felt a moment of panic.

The woman leaned a bit closer. "Don't you ever let anyone convince you it's wrong, dear. Being in love."

And off she hobbled, linking up again with her companion.

Too Young

Waking to the darkened ward with a nurse at her side.

"Bad dreams?" she asked quietly.

Charlie could only shiver and nod.

"It's to be expected after an accident. Don't be scared by them. If you have more and want to talk them away, just buzz. I won't mind."

But just how could she tell the nurse that she had murdered a man, lured him into a trap and pushed him back into freezing water to listen to his last words as he was dragged under by a pile of bricks and drowned?

I Get Ideas

The hardest day was when the fair pulled down and moved on. All the business with the doctors telling her she'd need to rest for four months and then ease herself back into physical work hadn't worried her. She would do as she pleased or, as she admitted to herself, what Miranda allowed. Besides, there was always other stuff she could do and the Wall had three riders. It was the thought of being on her own again that scared her. Even more than when Miranda hadn't talked to her for months. At least she had the others then and work to do. Now she would be with strangers in the hospital. And whilst the chance to read all day sounded good, it was already boring. Even the papers with all the news of the Festival of Britain.

"Don't look so glum or you'll set me off again," said Miranda. "Just think of the peace and quiet you'll have."

"Don't want it."

"Sulking won't help. And you won't be in here forever. Daisy's said I can have a week off when you go back to the house, just to get you settled."

Charlie grinned. The house was practically empty during the season. Virginia looked after the place. Her husband's family had run the boxing booth before the war, but her husband Michael hadn't survived Normandy and their boy Richard was not interested in joining the fair.

"Oh. Did you get some paper?"

"In the bag with the other stuff. And some pencils. Are you taking up drawing or something?"

"I want to see if I can work out a mechanism for your lorry so it all opens up easily. Cuts down on setting up time so I'll be able to get over and help put Old Tom up as well."

"I haven't even taken driving lessons yet. Haven't really had the time."

"My fault. Sorry."

"No it's not. Don't be silly. Bit scared to be honest."

"You'll be fine. I'll get you started. Make sure you have them booked for December and we'll get you through your test."

"Doesn't seem real. Me. Driving a lorry. I can't even climb trees."

"Just what do you think is involved in driving?"

"You know what I mean."

"I know I want to grab you," Charlie whispered.

Longing For You

The flapping of paper woke Charlie and she blinked in the late summer warmth, stretched and sighed. A breeze had caught the sketches she had made. She gathered them and tucked them away into the folder. There was nothing more she could do with them now until she was able to get to the lorry at Leatherhead.

She had spent the last week with Miranda at the house, fed and fussed over by Daisy's sister, Virginia. Much of the time, they had been in the warehouse, Charlie hobbling about and helping Miranda to set out the mirrors to get the best effect in the available space.

It hadn't been easy hefting the heavy distorting mirrors in their mahogany frames from one position to another, always worrying about the one that was missing, but they had laughed and grown more deeply in love with one another. And now Charlie lay on the old wooden garden bench, alone once more.

The day before, they had gone to the local hospital and the cast had been removed from Charlie's leg. She looked at it now, musing on the pale flesh and withered muscle.

"Sunlight," the doctor had said after studying the X-rays and pronouncing himself satisfied the leg was healed. "And gentle exercise."

She supposed, sourly, that seeing Miranda to the train station counted as exercise. Waving goodbye as she made her way to where the fair was currently pitched. Wandering back to the house to sit in the garden and look at the diagrams once more. Remembering that last kiss as they cut through the warehouse. Falling asleep on the bench.

All she wanted was to ride the Wall with the others, flirt with Miranda, steal a bit of time to read, all to the background of fairground life, blaring music, bright lights, crowds having a bit of fun. Instead she was sitting in a peaceful garden. She smiled to herself and picked up the nearest magazine, put it down again unopened.

Turn Back The Hands Of Time

The night was hungry, wrapped in deep impenetrable shadow. Buildings were festooned with icicles and frozen snow. Broken-boned ruins glimmered where they lay scattered by war.

With wraith-like silence and single purpose, she crossed the broken pavement and silent road, her breath smoking in whirling clouds that trailed behind her, curling, fading in the frosty air. Moving from moonlight to darkness she stayed with the deep shadows. And in her silent wake, just beyond the dying wisps of breath, other forms coalesced.

They were silent tonight, trailing without dance or play. They did not worry her any more, had long since become pale companions of the empty hours, thin reflections of the heart.

Waiting.

Softly, lightly, a whisper carrying with sibilant echo against the background of bombs.

"Donkey walks on four legs, and I walk on two, the last one I saw was just like you."

The shambling grotesque figure with its broken face stopped.

"Potato Pete is no good, chop him up for firewood, when he's dead, boil his head, make it into ginger bread."

"You did it, your tongue shall be slit, and all the dogs in the town shall have a little bit."

Keeping to the open, she danced and ran, the hard ring of his boots on the cobbles echoing in her ears as she turned a corner and out onto the bomb site. She slowed, chose her spot, and then stopped. As he came wheezing around the corner, she was facing him and he skidded on the icy surface, uncertain.

"Whistle while you work, the Warden tore her skirt, first he broke her, then he choked her, whistle while you work."

He charged, roaring.

Her feet slipped and she went down. Rough fingers grabbed and she kicked out, scrambling upright. Crossed the beam with her arms whirling above the darkness. She wrapped the rope round her hand, grabbed with the other and then heaved backwards with all the strength of blazing anger and sheer icy hatred.

He hit the ice and went straight through into the water beneath. Deep water.

From the deep cellar came the sound of ice squealing in protest and then cracking, of desperate breaths being drawn, of water splashing.

Then silence. A sudden rush of water.

A hand groping for a hold. A second hand appearing, finding a grip. The heel of her boots against the top of the wall. Water fountained into the moonlight. And then sloshed about in the deep cellar until the sound of broken ice and water was drowned by the distant bombing.

She tried to crawl away but could barely move, dragged down by a growing weight, fighting to draw air into her lungs, choking, dropping into frozen darkness with a silent scream. Dropping through into the scent of roses, waking to see the pink and yellow blooms that grew intertwined behind the bench.

"Are you all right, Chas?"

Charlie sat up as Virginia hurried down the garden path.

"You were calling out."

"Just a bad dream, Ginny. About the crash," she lied.

"I'll go and make a pot of tea. Nearly tea time, anyway."

"Be there in a minute. I'll just tidy up here."

She watched Virginia walk back toward the house wondering if she would ever be free of the nightmare. Picked up the magazines and bits of paper. Remembered something the nurse had said in hospital. Talk the dreams away. But there was no one she could tell, they wouldn't understand. And those that would, she could not burden with such knowledge or responsibility.

Perhaps if she wrote it down.

That evening, she sat up in bed and poured it out, her thoughts and ideas and feelings about the events scrawled on sheet after sheet of paper. It was jumbled, a mess, like pus from a wound. The wound still hurt after all these years, but maybe now the poison was drained it could heal.

If she lived that long. Because there, in her own handwriting, was a confession that could hang her. She stared at it for a long time, desperate to be free of it, scared what would happen if what she had written was read by anyone else, worried the police might one day arrest the wrong man.

She woke at first light to a chorus of sparrows, the garbled outpouring still clutched in her hand. When she returned from the bathroom, her leg aching, she smoothed out the creases, read what she had written and started all over again.

This time it was a straightforward telling of events as she knew them with as much detail as she could remember. What she had seen and when. A description of the man she knew only as 'Potato Pete'. An account of his death.

After dressing, she crept down to Daisy's office, cased up the typewriter and lugged it over to the warehouse where, wearing gloves, she pecked out her statement letter by letter. She folded the finished sheets and put them into a new envelope fresh from a new pack. She placed this in another envelope to keep it clean. She didn't suppose the police had her fingerprints on file, but she wasn't going to take any chances. She'd read enough Sexton Blakes to know how easy it was to slip up. The originals were torn into small pieces and she set fire to them in a metal hubcap, making sure they were all reduced to ash which she then ground to powder.

And then she brooded, not knowing what steps to take. She could send it to Scotland Yard, but it seemed too remote. What little she'd had to do with the police had been scary and there was always a deal of well-founded scepticism about them on the fairground.

There was one, though. The detective during the war who had taken the time to listen to her. Perhaps. She dug out her diary and found she had written his name, Detective Lock, probably because he'd been the first real detective she'd ever met.

It was easy enough to confirm he was still based locally, so she typed his name and address on an envelope, put her story in and sealed it. She was still undecided what to do about it, but had at least reached a point where she could relax, try to forget it, sleep without dreaming.

Cold, Cold Heart

Several days later, at lunch, Virginia had just cleared the table in the kitchen when she turned to Charlie.

"Do you know why Daisy would be writing to the local police?"

Charlie froze. All the care she'd taken and then to leave it on Daisy's desk.

"Oh well," Virginia continued. "I put a stamp on it and posted it this morning. Probably just forms or something."

The Last Degree

Feet Up

"Come on Ladies and Gents, lads and lasses, all the genuine thrills of the fair as the Indian Princesses ride the Wall of Death for your entertainment. And back with them today after playing knock and run on death's door, celebrating her twenty-first birthday, I give you Pine Leaf. So come on, part with your cash and make your way up to the gallery to see an all new show of daredevil stunts."

There was applause from the crowd in front of the booth as Charlie, riding the rollers, stood on the footplate of her bike and waved. Harry grinned as a queue began to form. It had been his idea to incorporate the accident into his spiel. That's what the punters were half hoping to see, he'd argued, and it was true. It wasn't really a brand new show, just the old one re-arranged with a few new stunts and a couple of wobbles thrown in to get the punters gasping.

That it was Charlie's twenty-first was a happy coincidence. And when she first rode up onto the wall, she was waving a large key cut out from hardboard and painted silver. And amidst all the clapping and loud music and the roar of the bikes, that first moment up on the Wall in front of a crowd was the first time she had felt at peace in more than half a year.

After her first solo run she sat and watched as the others did theirs, then rejoined them in various pairs, all three racing round together making Old Tom sway and some of the punters squeal. And then they finished on their set piece. Most riders rode the Wall anti-clockwise. Charlie was able to go both ways with ease. So Mary went up to the top and ran circuits there while Charlie found the mid line going the other way. And then Beth squeezed in on the bottom so that Charlie was the filling in the sandwich going in the opposite direction to the other two.

It drew deserved applause and sent the punters away happy.

Walking My Baby Back Home

“You’re limping. What happened? Are you all right?”

Miranda ambushed Charlie as she crossed from the Wall to where the riders’ bus was parked up.

“I’m fine, sweetheart. Just a bit sore. Come on in before the others get here.”

After a while, it began to dawn on Charlie that they’d had longer in the privacy of the bus than was usual. It was easy to be distracted when she had Miranda there, but in the end she began to worry. And feel hungry.

“Where have they got to?” she asked.

“Burning their identity cards?” suggested Miranda.

“More likely building a bomb shelter.” They shivered.

Stepping out of the bus into the dark was eerie.

“Surely they can’t still be closing up the Wall,” said Miranda.

Everywhere else was quiet. Shutters were up. Lights were off. The only signs of life came from the living vans where suppers were being cooked and eaten and someone was struggling along with a can of water filled at the standpipe.

As they approached Old Tom a bike coughed and then roared within.

“What are they playing at?” asked Charlie.

Miranda shrugged.

They made their way round the back of the show where the shadows were darkest and Charlie opened the door to the interior. It was pitch dark inside.

“What are you lot playing at?” she called.

Lights blazed and Miranda pushed her inside to a chorus of “Surprise!”

Charlie spun around, surrounded by cheers and catcalls from the gallery along with cries of ‘Happy Birthday!’, to see Miranda with a huge grin on her face dancing up and down on the spot.

Takes Two To Tango

It was a warm, close evening and the field where they were pitched was baked solid. The schools holidays had started and the fair was swamped with families. Charlie was taking a much needed breather from the fumes in Old Tom, standing in the shadows by the penny machines tent watching Miranda as she collected money and handed out the wooden hoops on her parents' stall.

Harry walked past, back-pedalled, and sidled up to Charlie, taking an undue interest in the penny machine beside her.

"What's up?"

"Policeman looking for you," said Harry which explained why he was shielding her from view. "Do you need time to leg it?"

"Me?" She peered over his shoulder. "Where?"

He glanced over his shoulder "That bloke in an old suit with his back to us, over by the coconuts."

Charlie picked him out. "How do you know he's a policeman?"

Harry looked at her with one eyebrow raised. "Don't be daft, girl."

She smiled. The man turned and spoke to a woman. Charlie saw his face. Drew a sudden breath. It was Lock.

"You all right? You just nip in the back of the ghost train. We'll all swear blind we never heard of you."

Barely able to speak she said: "No. No it's all right. Get Lorna to stand in for me will you?"

Harry gave her a searching look and then nodded before wandering off.

With her heart trying to gouge its way out of her chest, Charlie wove through the crowds until she was standing beside the detective who was still talking and laughing with the woman.

He sensed her standing there and turned.

"You wanted to see me?" she asked.

He looked at her for a moment and then touched the woman's arm. She looked first at him and then at Charlie. There was the hint of a sigh and then a smile.

"Won't be a few minutes," he said, and then walked away from the coconut shy with Charlie following.

"Is there somewhere we can talk without being overheard?" Lock asked.

Charlie nodded, too choked with fear to be able to talk; her head filled with the thought she might never see Miranda again, that she would hate her for keeping a secret, hate her for what she had done.

Impervious to the crowds, her head spinning, she made a bee-line for the compound with the living vans and led Lock to the Wall of Death bus.

She unlocked the door and turned to see the detective looking at the beautifully painted side of the living quarters.

"You ride the Wall?"

She nodded and ushered him in. He pulled an envelope from an inside pocket of his jacket, removed several typewritten sheets of paper. Held them up with a raised eyebrow.

"How… How did you know it was me?" she asked, finding her voice as she closed the door.

He squeezed himself onto the bench behind the table, took off his hat.

"I didn't. Not for a long time. And please. Sit. Relax."

Charlie stayed where she was. Lock shrugged.

"You remembered my name after all these years?" he asked.

"Tom told me. I wrote it in my diary."

"Tom? Ah, yes. The old man who came to your rescue. Was sorry to hear he'd passed. A good sort."

"So how did you know it was me?"

"Like I said, it took a long time for the penny to drop. I couldn't think why this had been sent to me," he said tapping the sheets of paper. "It wasn't a case I had anything to do with outside reading about it in the Police Gazette and making sure my mob were keeping their eyes open. It puzzled me for months. In fact I'd filed it and forgotten about it until something reminded me of the raid on the warehouse and the young girl who helped me in the spring of 1944."

Charlie shivered, conscious of the presence of five ghostly figures watching. Somehow. In the cramped space. She saw the detective frown as well; pull his jacket a bit tighter.

"What will happen to me?" asked Charlie.

"Nothing."

"But…"

He tapped the sheets of paper. "There's no evidence you did this. No…" he paused for a moment looking round the interior of the bus with a slight frown. "No witnesses."

"Don't you believe it?"

"Yes. Every word. I can't imagine how terrified you must have been. You were what? Thirteen? And you did it to save your friend. I looked into the case. Officially it's unsolved, but by the time William Albert Bonwick – that's your Potato Pete's real name – by the time he died he was already in the frame and the killings stopped. All you did was cheat the hangman out of his ten quid. There's nothing to be served by dragging it all out again, reopening the parents' wounds, pulling you through the courts only to have a lawyer get you off. Which he would. I don't for one second condone vigilante justice, but it sounds to me more like it was self-defence. Against a truly nasty bastard. So. Consider yourself told off. Ever try it again…" He looked at her standing there. Studied her. "No. But you wouldn't would you."

Charlie let a tear roll and the detective pretended he hadn't noticed, fishing in his pockets for something.

"How you had the courage to send it in I'll never know."

"I didn't." said Charlie. "I'd had bad dreams ever since and they were getting worse. I wrote it down to try and get rid of them. Typed it out cos…"

"A confession in your handwriting." He nodded.

"I got as far as putting it in an envelope. Then someone else found it and posted it thinking it was forms for the fair."

He picked up the sheets of paper and handed them to Charlie. "You can rest easy. There are no copies." He finally pulled a box of matches from his pocket and put it on the table.

It was a long time after Lock had gone before her hand was steady enough to strike a match. In the gloom of the cramped interior she watched as each sheet burned and curled to a dark crisp, dropping them one by one into the small sink before sluicing the ashes away with water.

“What did he want?” asked Mary when they caught up with Charlie, heading for Miranda’s booth.

“Not carted you off then?” chimed in Beth.

“Shut up you lot.”

Miranda’s intervention was met with a chorus of raspberries.

“No,” said Charlie. “He… You remember when there was a raid on the warehouse up the street from ours?”

They looked blank.

“In ’44.”

They all nodded.

“I was watching from one of the empty houses across the street, got hauled out by a copper. Tom came to the rescue. Said I was family.”

“And?”

“That was the detective in charge. He’s here with his family. Remembered the name. Just being curious.”

“Nosy, more like,” said Beth. “Seems a bit odd him just turning up.”

George appeared, curious to know what the conference was about. He listened as Charlie repeated her lie. “You’ll find the whole world and his dog pass through the fair. If you stand around watching for long enough.”

They took the hint and headed back to Old Tom for the next show.

Charlie lingered a moment. Miranda’s presence calmed her.

“And all they ever see,” continued George, “is the shiny façade, the little worlds of wonder we create for them.”

It wasn’t much of a smile, but she managed one. “I think I prefer the world in the shadows behind the light.”

Faith Can Move Mountains

Bright islands, somnolent in the sun. Scrub covered hill peaks breaching the shallow sea. Wind sculpted. Quiet. Clear waters teeming with life. A ship anchored in the sound.

Obliterated by light that seared through her soul to be replaced by roiling, scalding thunder, shaking ground, a rain of twisted metal, the speeding wave…

To wake with a wordless shout, the image of the towering mud-laden fingers reaching out from the fireball, consuming the light, blotting out the sun, casting a vast and poisonous shadow across the future.

As Miranda folded her into her arms and whispered soothing sounds, all Charlie could see were the floating corpses of thousands of turtles washing onto a beach.

The Ravell'd Sleeve

Side By Side

"I'm never going to get the hang of it. Feel such an idiot."

"Don't be so hard on yourself, Em. This is a small field. It was a tight turn and the ground is soft. Pass that pin."

"I should have known all that."

"And you only passed your test a few months ago. Unhitch."

"But I've been practising…"

Miranda paused as they lowered one side of her trailer using a small hand winch, watching with satisfaction as it settled firmly into place.

"You'll get all the practice you need now the mirrors are on the road."

"I hope they're all right." Miranda glanced at the padded forms at the far end of the trailer.

"They'll be fine. Hand me that locking bar."

Charlie took the bar and shoved it through her belt so it would be to hand.

"At least we can do this bit all right."

They grinned at each other, took hold of the hinged wall and raised it up part way onto props. Fixing the canvas roof was tricky as they had to work underneath, threading a cable through rings on the wall and loops in the canvas. In the gloom, they shared a quick kiss and then carried on with their work, fixing first one side of the trailer and then the other, creating a space for Miranda's mirrors.

With the sides locked in place and the roof up, Charlie made a last round of the trailer to check everything was secure.

"Right," she said quietly, satisfied that all was well, "I'll just check the legs outside again and then head over to Old Tom. See you later, sweetheart."

"Take care."

Miranda watched Charlie skip down the steps to the grass of the field and then made her way to the rear of the trailer where the mirrors were packed. It was scary. Her very own show.

Miranda's Magical Maze of Mirrors with a vibrant new sign from Fred Fowle hanging over the entrance. She knew she'd be in debt for years, paying off the loan for the lorry. She didn't care. Not with Charlie there to help.

She unlaced the padded cover and stripped it away from the first mirror, unhitched it from its anchor point, and ran it on its rollers to the welded rings on the floor where she padlocked it in place. The work kept her from worrying about Charlie who would, by now, be helping to put up the Wall. It was the most dangerous part of their work, that and pulling down. More people were injured each year shifting the fair from site to site than during any novelty act.

All The Time And Everywhere

"Oi!"

Charlie grinned at Eric as she popped the purloined chip into her mouth.

"Shouldn't you be helping Kath?"

"She's all right," said Eric, moving his chips out of reach. "Tent's up. Cases in place. Just unpacking now. We'll be inside with our feet up while you're still putting that monstrosity of yours together."

Charlie managed to help herself to another chip and passed along the front of the tent. Butterworth & Sabin's Cabinet of Wonders. She'd pop in sometime in the week as they had a new exhibit. A genuine meteorite from outer space. She'd tried to point out that meteorites didn't come from anywhere else, but Eric had replied that he knew what the punters wanted.

The gallopers were all lit up and blasting out a tune. As ever they were by the entrance, all set to entice people in and excite them with all their colour, movement, and traditional fairground music.

David was finally back on the hoopla stall. He'd been put in hospital over Christmas by the awful smog and everyone had feared for his life. He still looked frail, especially swathed in layers of clothing. But he was glad to be back on the road, even if he was constantly fussed over by Daisy who forever demanded to know where his aminophylline tablets were.

From elsewhere on the site, Doris Day was singing 'When I Fall in Love'. Rob and Paul were standing at the base of one of the speaker poles staring balefully up at a fuzzy crackling sound, discussing what the problem was and how they were going to fix it.

"Nice of you to show up," said Beth with a wink when Charlie arrived at the site of the Wall. The base was already down and level on its bed of sleepers and Harry, in the cab of their truck, was operating the crane to lift the first vertical section of Old Tom.

Charlie pulled on heavy gloves and joined the others as they pushed the dangling section of the Wall into place, shoving props against it until it could be bolted to successive pieces.

It was a long, hard job. Food was brought out to them as they worked in the failing light of day and they ate as they worked, needing to get the structure complete and the canvas roof on to protect the riding surface from rain.

As always, they were the last to finish, with others drifting in to help, especially with the canvas roof. Close to midnight, Harry saw Mary and Beth back to the bus they now had to themselves and escorted Lorna back to the Cutwood van to say his goodnights. Charlie was left to her own devices and was grateful. She had come to enjoy these few moments alone in the dark with the sleeping fair as she trudged back to the van she now shared with Miranda.

There was a ritual to setting up. It began with a convocation of owners and shareholders gathered in the centre of the site. They talked partly in cant, partly in a verbal shorthand that referred to the specific site, the weather, time of year, their knowledge of previous fairs on the site. From this they drew up a diagram on the ground, marking out the centres of each attraction which were then zealously guarded by acolytes.

Once the murmuring, bartering, and marking out had finished, there was a fixed order in which lorries arrived to decant the skeleton of each attraction, bases made of railway sleepers and other old timbers being laid and made level with props and wedges. Then the bones were erected and bolted together, forming gaunt frameworks against the afternoon sky.

At the same time, generators were being coupled to the miles of cable that snaked along behind the attractions, to be fed into each ride and sideshow as the viscera were inserted: the engines and electrics, the lights and sound, the little back ways and hidey-holes where the owners would sit and operate their magic. Then fleshed over with canvas and board, brightly painted and lit. All decked out with red, white and blue bunting this year for the upcoming coronation.

The whole operation was carried out to the sound of hammering and shouting and good natured banter, spirits often dampened by the rain but never washed away. And once everything was ready and tested and locked up, the weary magicians could retire for the night, leaving their creatures ready for the morrow when the animating spark of the generators would jerk each of them to brash wakefulness and the life blood that was the flow of punters would course in the veins of the fair.

For now, though, there was relative silence. The rustle of canvas in the night breeze, the muted sound of a radio from a living van. The smell of churned up turf and diesel on the chill air. Shadows. Anticipation.

At their cramped little living van behind the cab of Miranda's lorry, Charlie washed and collapsed in to her bunk, was asleep by the time Miranda crawled in beside her.

Where The Winds Blow

"Have they finished yet?"

"For the most part. The uniformed bobby got bored. Wandered off. But the blokes from the Council are still at the Russ stall. They can't believe it isn't fixed."

"Bastards. I mean. George Russ, of all people. Straight as a die."

"Yeah. Well the bloke from the Council couldn't get the hoop over a prize and a box and reckons George was using smaller hoops. So George stood there with the hoops that had been measured and got every one of them over first time. So the bloke from the Council looked an idiot, which he is, so now he wants to see their books and everything."

"Bet that went down well."

"George told him straight that his books were examined once a year by an accountant and his returns submitted to the tax people and that if the man from the Council wanted a look he'd have to get the police to arrest him and issue a search warrant."

"Good for George. Bet Daisy's spitting blood. Typical bloody Council. The other one's gone to look for the bobby they came with."

"Typical bloody Council."

"I just said that."

"Yeah. Well it's worth repeating. Where'd they think we get our permits from in the first place if not from them? And then they've got the nerve to turn up and question us."

Charlie moved on from the Bingo tent, leaving Judith and Gail to their conversation. They'd had the Wall inspected that morning and given the all clear although no one really knew what authority these people had. But they could refuse a licence for the fair in future years so everyone felt compelled to play along.

Now the fair was full of punters. She'd just finished a show and was crossing the fairground to the mirrors to see how Miranda was doing. Especially as there had been trouble here last year with local yobs. Perhaps, she thought, the Council were blaming it on the fair. It wouldn't be the first time. It wouldn't be the last.

At least the locals weren't staying away, filling the fair with noise and laughter, the young ones handing over pennies they'd saved, older ones with a bit of loose silver in their pockets.

Threading her way between stalls, still in her riding gear, Charlie stepped back to let a couple pass, looking for a moment into the face of the woman. It was a quickly exchanged glance and they both continued on their respective ways. Long seconds followed as memory drew the lines and coloured in the spaces between past and present.

Charlie stopped and turned to see the woman had done the same. They were just a few steps apart. Her whole body felt electrified. They spoke simultaneously.

"Mave?"

"Charlie?"

For long, breathless, tearful seconds they hugged and jumped up and down. Held each other at arms length. Embraced again. Looked each other up and down.

"Wait here," said Charlie. "Don't move I'll be right… No."

She grabbed Mavis by the hand.

"Come with me."

Mavis in turn grabbed her partner and they let themselves be led through the crowds.

At the Wall they stopped and Charlie called up to Lorna. "Can you do the next show for me?"

"What's it worth?"

"Packet of peanuts for a monkey."

Lorna stuck out her tongue and grinned.

"You ride bikes on the Wall of Death?" asked a horrified Mavis.

Charlie grinned at her, a little girl again. She nodded.

Mavis looked up at the metal web that enclosed the Wall, the gaudy banner across the front proclaiming the Indian Princesses, Lorna grinning down at them as she stood beside one of the Indian bikes. Mavis nodded.

"You always were a daredevil. But you look well. Oh. I can't believe it. We…" And she started to cry.

Her partner handed her a clean handkerchief, a bemused look on his face.

"Where's my manners?" asked Mavis. "This is my husband, Will. Will, this is Charlie. The little girl I thought we'd lost." She began to cry again and Charlie had to wipe her own eyes with the back of her hand.

"Come on," she said. "I'll brew us some tea. We'll use the coach as my van is tiny."

It meant nothing to them, but they followed anyway, Charlie explaining that the serene, honey-haired beauty in the kiosk for the Magical Mirror Maze was her very best friend Miranda.

They passed between two sideshow tents and into the living compound. A couple of faces appeared in windows, nodded to Charlie and faded away. At the coach, Charlie led them up the steps to the interior.

"We keep the bikes in the back when we travel. There are bunks."

She grabbed the kettle and filled it, the gas popping once the match caught.

"Is this where you live?" asked Mavis.

"I did. Not any more. I share a van with Em. Miranda. It's easier. More room for the girls here, for one thing. And I help Em with her mirrors."

She could see Mavis and William looking round, conscious of the cramped space.

"Besides. It's only when we're on the road. Rest of the time we're in the house in Southwark."

"But what happened. I saw you were limping. Was that…?"

"I came a cropper on the Wall the year before last. Just a few broken bones, that's all."

"That's all? And what about…? I don't even know where to start."

"How about with some tea?" asked Charlie, pouring from the pot. She added a dash of condensed milk to each mug from a can. "Bit on the rough side."

"I suppose you'll have to get back to work."

"Lorna will cover for a few shows. We often do that."

"Are you happy, Charlie? Doing all this?"

"Yes. These people took me in when… They are family. I love being on the road. I have friends. A home."

"I want to know everything."

Charlie cast a glance at the silent, bemused Will. "So do I."

They laughed

"You must come to tea. Can you get away for an afternoon?"

"Council here won't let us open on Sunday."

"That's settled then. Come early. After lunch." Mavis opened her handbag and pulled out a little notebook. She wrote and then tore out the page. "Our address. It's on the High Street. Not far. The flat's above the shop. You'll see."

Broken Wings

She did see.

Sunday afternoon. All scrubbed up by Miranda, she had been sent on her way in her best trousers and jacket, with a box of chocolates and a bunch of flowers. She had tried to persuade Miranda to come with her, but Miranda wanted to clean her mirrors. Charlie didn't push the point. Miranda was shy at the best of times. How she coped with the public was a constant source of wonder.

And what Charlie saw was a smart little shop, Reid & Thompson, selling electrical goods and offering installation and repairs. Next to which was a discreet door. She pressed the bell, heard a faint buzzing, footsteps descending.

The door opened and Will stood there smiling.

"Come on in, Charlie. I can't tell you how excited she's been. I'll lead the way."

Up narrow stairs into a bright flat where Mavis was waiting on the landing. They embraced and Charlie felt seven years old again, a feeling compounded when she was ushered into the living room to find Audrey waiting there.

When the tears had been dried and the men shunted off to the kitchen, the three sat and stared at each other for a while. They could hear the rumble of voices, the sound of children giggling.

"We have to ask what happened," said Audrey. "Are you up to it? Talking about it?"

Charlie took a deep breath and nodded.

"I took a bus. To the docks. As far as it would go, anyway. Asked at a tea van how I could get to the Customs House. One of the men there who'd been helping clear rubble, he took me. We got as far as where Nan caught her bus home. Saw it by the side of the road. Peeled apart by a bomb. There were rows of bodies on the pavement. Covered with blankets, heads covered, feet sticking out. I saw Nan's shoes. Her best blue ones. You remember? All scuffed, they were. Her stockings torn."

It had been years now that the grief had found no proper channel. Until that Sunday afternoon. Mavis and Audrey either side holding her as she howled and sobbed for everything that was lost.

"I suppose that's what saved us," said Mavis. "You going off like that. We were both out looking for you when the bomb fell on the school. Down by your Nan's house, we were, thinking you might be there."

"We searched for weeks, Charlie."

"We must have been passing each other in the streets," said Charlie, "but I thought you must be dead and it was all my fault."

"No. No. You poor child. I 'spect we've all felt guilty over the years," said Audrey. "I know we did. But we couldn't stay any longer. Our factory got moved and we had to go with it. Still came back when we could on our days off. And then when it was all over, there was Will and Chris. They'd both been electricians as well. In the factory. We got together. Started the shop. The boys go out and about. Put up aerials. Install the televisions. We run the shop and do repairs. And then there's the kids. But what about you? Where did you go? Did the fairground people take you in?"

Charlie told them. Most of it. The years fending for herself. Finding the Simmons.

"No wonder you are so grown up. I couldn't have done it."

"Me neither."

"I found her grave," Charlie said, gripping the soggy handkerchief. "The headstone?"

"That was Aud and me."

"I should pay you for that."

"You will do no such thing, Charlie Cornelius," said Audrey. "It was the least we could do. She was a good woman, your

Nan. Looked out for us. Made a good job of you as well from the look of you. Not sure what she'd make of the motorbikes and all, but she'd be so proud of you. All grown up. Looking after yourself."

They all cried a bit more, leeching away some of the sadness that had tarnished their lives.

Both women had glanced toward the door and the sound of children playing elsewhere. After faces were washed, Charlie half expecting one of them to wield a washcloth, tea was eaten in the chaos of two families, with children and spouses properly introduced. Charlie fielded questions about boyfriends with a plea of being too busy for that sort of thing, feeling guilty all the while.

"And your friend?" asked Mave. "Did she not want to come?"

Charlie blushed. "Em's very shy."

"She's lucky to have you for a friend then," said Aud.

They talked long into the evening, untangling painful knots and weaving a little happiness into their memories. And when Charlie finally went home, kicking through old newspaper chip wrappings with their grease-stained nuclear-test headlines, it was with a small photograph album that Audrey and Mavis had made of all the pictures they could find of their time at Gertrude's house – pictures of themselves, of their room, of Charlie, of Gertie. She held the album tight as she walked through the quiet, Sunday streets back to the fair and the warm embrace of the present.

Wish You Were Here

Charlie stopped so suddenly on the path that Miranda walked right into her.

"What is it? You all right?"

"I…"

Charlie looked at her watch. It was ten past nine. They'd just finished their breakfast and had left the house, making for the warehouse to spend the day with the mirrors, checking them over, touching up the paintwork. It was the ideal day. Mild and dry, even though it was late November.

"Charlie?"

"Sorry, Em. It's like someone walked over my…"

"Grave?"

"Yes. No. It was like that, but… different. Opposite?"

"Too much sugar on your porridge, if you ask me."

Daisy watched them through the kitchen window as they ran off laughing, just like they had as children. She sighed. There was altogether too much growing up going on in the world.

Smile Of Light

Little Things Mean A Lot

Wraith-like, steam from the mugs wisped away as Charlie climbed the shadowy back stairs. At the top, she edged her way through the servant's door, pushing it closed behind her with a foot. The landing always made her shiver when she was alone. Even now, the memory of that encounter with the one-legged Tom who went to his death to save her was strong and clear. The few steps to the bedroom door echoed through several pasts and futures and left her ever grateful for the presence of Miranda.

She put her own mug on the chest of drawers just inside the door and crossed to where Miranda was sitting, placing the other on the small writing desk in front of the picture postcard of a raven, dropping a light kiss on top of Miranda's bowed head. The scratching of the pen stopped and Miranda straightened.

"Thanks," she said as put the top on her pen and set it down in the centre fold of her ledger so she could warm her hands on the mug. She was wrapped in a large blanket, a scarf round her neck, feet resting on a stone hot water bottle.

"Snowing again," said Charlie from the depths of her great-coat as she stood by the window and stared out into the grey world beyond.

"I've nearly finished this. Just need to put the last address in and we can get out and post the letters."

"Who is it this time?"

"Several companies in Birmingham. Not sure it's worth it any more."

"Until next time."

"But I'm running out of ideas. I'm almost at the end of the list I got from the Guild."

"Someone must have made the mirrors."

"I know, but we've been over them a dozen times and not found a maker's mark. Great great granny Elizabeth didn't leave any letters. Least, none I've ever heard of. Alice didn't have any or she'd have passed them on."

"We'll keep looking."

"But I don't know where. GG granny E surely wouldn't have gone too far to get them made. Even Birmingham is stretching things."

Miranda sighed and turned back to her ledger. She copied in the last address, blotted the entry, and closed the book. Sipping her tea, she looked across at Charlie where she sat on the edge of Miranda's bed.

A sudden explosion of noise made them turn to the door as a two of the younger members of family burst in, arguing loudly and trying to exchange blows.

"Get out," yelled Miranda in her best fairground voice.

The two stopped mid fight and stood frozen for a second before scrambling out of the room.

"Bloody kids," muttered Miranda into her tea. "No privacy in this place."

Charlie winked and Miranda smiled. "They won't be back in a hurry. I nearly ran away as well."

Miranda stuck her tongue out.

The Finger Of Suspicion

They skated with glee down the icy side path that the younger members of the family had made into a slide before Daisy could get out with the salt. And then they stomped off up the hill, wrapped in coats and scarves and balaclavas and gloves, puffing clouds into the still air, scooping up fresh snow and throwing it at one another as if they were still just youngsters themselves.

It was busy on the High Street despite the cold. Great, shapeless cocoons shuffled back and forth, stamping snow from their feet as they went into shops. The Post Office was busy as well and Charlie and Miranda queued patiently. At the counter they were served by the as-ever neatly turned out Mr Michaels, his only concession to the cold being a woollen muffler and a pair of fingerless mitts.

“Good morning, Miss Russ,” he said. “Miss Cornelius. What can I do for you?”

“Can I have a dozen tupenny ha’penny stamps please?”

Mr Michaels pulled the stamp book toward him, opened the cover and ran a finger down the worn tabs, opening it at the correct section. He tore off a small block of red stamps with the face of the new queen on them. Miranda handed over a half crown, tucking the stamps safely in a compartment of her purse.

There were dancing flurries of snow in the air as they crossed quickly to the sweet and baccy shop to get some rose creams for Daisy. Back outside they were passing the ruins of a shop on the edge of a bomb site when Charlie’s hand shot out. Miranda turned, feeling a tug at her coat and looked down to see that Charlie had caught someone in the act of trying to pick her pocket. Someone small and, now, very worried looking.

“You little—” began Miranda but stopped when she saw the expression on Charlie’s face. For a second it worried her, serious and troubled, and then it cleared and Charlie winked. She hauled the youngster off the pavement and onto the bomb site, Miranda following.

“Who’s keeping watch?” asked Charlie of the youngster who was swathed in scarves and peered out through a gap between them and a thick, woolly hat. “I know there’s someone else here.”

Miranda looked round. There were dozens of places to hide although they would all be cold.

“Or are you thinking of sneaking off and leaving… him?”

“Wouldn’t do that.”

An equally small figure appeared as if directly from the thin, cold air. Charlie peered and then grinned.

“Bloody ‘ell,” said the newly arrived character. “It’s me. Brasso. Do you remember?”

“And how is…” Charlie never had known the name of their leader.

“Er ladyship? She’s fine. Though she’ll be livid when she ‘ears Prestcold ‘ere got isself caught.”

Others began to emerge.

"Special circumstances, Brasso. Tell her who it was. And you lot," she added, looking slowly round at the group of urchins. "Remember my face. Remember Miranda's. We're off limits. Anyone else we're with, you can chance your arm, but they won't be as forgiving as me."

Charlie turned back to face Brasso and winked, ignoring the whispered questions that were passing back and forth, words like 'fossil', 'oldies', 'should be in a museum', 'caught you didn't they?' mixed in with bits she couldn't catch. Brasso snapped his fingers and silence fell like a stone.

"Sorry about that. Rude lot. Anyway, we'd best be off."

"Give my regards to—"

"Will do," said Brasso, cutting in as he turned and herded the newer members of his tribe back into the shadows.

"Don't get caught," said Charlie and grinned as she saw two fingers raised in her direction just before Brasso vanished.

Miranda stood open mouthed. "Were they…?"

Charlie nodded and then said, "Come on, I've had an idea."

"Hang out the flags."

Am I A Toy Or A Treasure

Without really thinking about it or needing it, the first thing Miranda did when sitting down was to wipe the condensation from the window. Charlie dropped into the seat next to her as the bus pulled away. She delved in a pocket and then held up a few coppers.

"You're splashing the cash, aren't you?" asked Miranda. "Where you getting it all?"

She was glad that Charlie was paying, wherever they were going. It was always harder in the off season.

"I'm not spending it all on stamps," replied Charlie.

"That's not fair."

"You just spent half a dollar on them when you said you couldn't think of anyone else to write to."

"Well, where *are* we going? What's this idea of yours?"

Charlie was happy for Miranda to change the subject. She'd been unfair about the stamps. The mirrors were important and the fact that one was missing was a constant irritant in Miranda's life. But before she could answer, the clippie swayed alongside.

"Two to Elephant and Castle, please," said Charlie, handing over the money. The clippie checked and dropped the pennies into her satchel, slid out two tickets and punched them, handed them over and moved on.

"Why are we going there?"

"So we can go somewhere else."

"Charlie!"

"You got your list of mirror makers from the Showmen's Guild, right?"

Miranda nodded. "What of it?"

"What if there's a Mirror Maker's Guild? Or someone who knows all about the history of mirror making?"

"Suppose so. But how do we find them."

"Like I said, I had a thought."

When the bus arrived at Elephant and Castle, Charlie grabbed Miranda's hand and pulled her along the busy pavement. They fetched up on the kerb for a moment before Charlie wove them through the traffic to the accompaniment of small squeals from Miranda. She was used to it, but still gave Charlie a glare.

"Now where are we going?"

"Somewhere warm to start with."

Miranda followed Charlie into the Underground Station ticket hall and caught up with her as she turned away from the window, tickets in hand.

"What's wrong?" she asked, worried by the confusion on Charlie's face.

"It's all wrong," Charlie mumbled looking round. "I could have sworn you went that way," she added with a nod of her head.

"When were you last here, then?"

"Ten years ago."

"Come off it. I can't even remember what I had for dinner yesterday."

They made their way down to the Bakerloo Line, Charlie's head full of unsettling memories, of the people she had met, serving tea and buns, their own tea party afterwards, a whole world within and beneath the world.

Down on the platform, Miranda pushed Charlie to a bench jutting from the wall. "You don't look well."

"I'll be fine," said Charlie, building a smile that did nothing to convince Miranda. "I was just… I was down here for days. I think. When all the V1s starting dropping. But it all seems… turned around. Even this bench. I'm sure… Oh, never mind."

Miranda grabbed Charlie's hand and gave it a quick squeeze and this time the smile was real. She knew her memory wasn't at fault, it was just that she was no longer sure what nature of thing it was she remembered – actual events, dreams, a looking glass reality, or something else.

A train drew in and they boarded, changed at Charing Cross to the Northern Line and re-emerged into the cold and grey streets at Tottenham Court Road. And before long Miranda knew where they were going, staring up at the grey columns of the façade of the British Museum.

"We can't go in there," said Miranda.

"Why not? It's open to the public. It's where all the people who might know about mirrors are."

They went up the steps and between the columns, finding themselves in the entrance hall. Even Charlie felt intimidated, but she dealt with it in her own way. Head on. When she spotted a uniformed attendant, crossing between visitors, she intercepted him, Miranda in tow.

"We'd like to talk to someone about mirrors, please."

The attendant, white moustache bristling, looked them up and down and said, with a sniff, "This ain't a pawn shop."

With that, he marched off.

"One is often tempted to violence where Evers is concerned, but it would only lead to trouble."

They turned, Charlie unclenching her fists, to find themselves face to face with a young woman about their own age.

"My name's Olive. Olive Driver. Let me apologise on behalf of the Museum. And let me make amends, if I can. You were asking about mirrors?"

Charlie introduced them and then nudged Miranda who stuttered out an explanation.

"But that's fascinating. How long have you been looking?"

"About eight or nine years," replied Miranda.

"Gosh. Right. Well, this is outside the BM's remit. You'd do better at the V and A." She read their faces as she spoke. "Come on. It's nearly my lunch hour. I'll take you and introduce you. Someone there is bound to be able to help."

Rain, Rain, Rain

From the moment they left the station it was clear the place had changed. And when they reached the street they were heading for, it was presented in spades. Despite being outwardly the same, they felt that the cheery, thumbs-up, stuff-you-Adolf attitude built up during the privation of the war years and so beloved of propagandists and film makers had long since been dissipated. Developers had squabbled over the area and left it in limbo. People had moved out, it had become dusty and tired and forgotten until there was no spirit left to resist the creeping rot of dodgy dealers, shady garages and workshops, wide boys, spivs, race track gangs and all the other riff-raff who had the police in their cash-filled pockets.

Private clubs and gang houses filled the empty properties and the weary locals kept their curtains closed and their children off the streets, especially their daughters. There was rarely trouble, but only because the locals knew they had no protection from the police and the gangs had bigger fish to fry in other parts of town.

As they made their way along the street, a leaning Cosh Boy peeled himself away from his doorway to slouch on the pavement. Charlie and Miranda exchanged a quick glance. They weren't impressed by the spotty faced dandy with his velvet collar and elaborately greased hair. They were two a penny on the fairground and rarely caused trouble if they were alone.

Long before they reached him, they stopped and knocked on a door.

When it opened, they both stepped back.

"Hello," said the young woman. "You must be Miranda and Charlie? Come on in. Mum's in the kitchen."

There was a spread of sandwiches already on the table and the gas was lit with a pop under the kettle as they stepped into the kitchen. Mrs Baker turned and smiled.

"You've met Maureen, then. I hope you didn't have no bother coming down from the station. Brighton's gone downhill these last couple of years. Awful now it is. A body's not safe out there any more."

Charlie and Miranda could see Maureen behind her mother pulling a half-amused, half-exasperated face. Later, when they were dizzy with the landlady's monologue and stuffed full of sandwiches and cake, Maureen led them up to their room.

"Same one," she said. "Mum insisted. Won't let me decorate, neither. She took it hard when dad died."

Even in the grey afternoon light, the white room felt bright and open.

"Is it as bad round here now as she says?" asked Miranda.

"We saw some of your native wildlife," added Charlie.

"Spotty Cosh Boy up the road?"

They nodded.

"That'll be Jim," explained Maureen. "He's local. Acts tough but couldn't fight his way out of a wet paper bag. There are one or two really unsavoury types who've moved in, though. Buying up the workshops mostly. God alone knows what for. But the area is run down. The war. Years of rationing. We're all tired. And mum will probably give up letting rooms, although she'll keep this one for the likes of you."

"You live local?" asked Miranda.

"Portslade for now. I visit mum a couple of times a week. She doesn't like to go out much now. I'll likely move back here at some stage." She almost kept the sigh from her voice. "Still, never mind that. Sorry about the weather."

Charlie shrugged. "It's the only reason we could get away. The field we were meant to set up in was flooded and the fair cancelled. So we thought a long weekend away would cheer us up."

They all had a good laugh about that as rain beat against the window.

"Oh well," said Maureen. "Plenty to do in town if you run fast. You have yourselves a nice break. Usual arrangement," she added, handing over the front door key.

How Do You Speak To An Angel?

From the shelter over the seats down the centre of the West Pier, they watched the rain. As they were pretty much alone, they huddled together holding hands still sticky from the doughnuts they'd eaten.

"Do you think it'll ever stop?" asked Miranda.

It stopped raining.

"How did you do that?" asked Charlie.

"I don't know, but shall we go into town?"

With an eye on the clouds, they strode along the pier, running their hands on the wet handrails to wash away the sugar. King's Road was just as deserted as the pier had been. Gloomy faces peered out of the lounge windows of the Metropole and other hotels as they passed.

Half way to the Palace Pier they crossed the road. More rain threatened so they threaded their way up Middle Street, past the synagogue on one side and then the Spotted Dog pub on the other. They sheltered for a moment beneath the canopy outside the Hippodrome when a nasty squall dumped more rain. When they reached Duke Street, they turned right and made their way to the Ship Street Post Office.

Dripping in line, they queued for stamps and Miranda posted some more letters to mirror making companies on her much expanded list. Charlie dropped a postcard to the Princesses in the box, along with Miranda's card to her family.

When they emerged, it seemed a little brighter so, fortified by the sandwiches Mrs Baker had insisted on making for them, they wandered into The Lanes. These dozen or so byways were a tiny labyrinth that seemed to expand the deeper you explored. Tiny, dark shops lined the narrow alleys, windows heaped with antiques, books, jewellery, and myriad reflections of Charlie and Miranda who stared back and sometimes waved and smiled.

Now and then faces would appear from within, curious about the laughing young women, one them scowling beside a shaken fist. In the end they got lost, Charlie convinced they had already been along one lane, Miranda insisting they hadn't and dragging Charlie with her.

By this stage, Charlie's attention had wandered from the shop wonders into which Miranda still peered avidly. Instead, she contented herself with watching Miranda and falling in love all over again as a wisp of her honey coloured hair worked its way loose from her woolly hat.

On the pretence of peering into the window at whatever had caught Miranda's attention, she pushed close up beside her. Miranda leaned against her.

"What have you seen?"

"Nothing," said Miranda, just as Charlie spotted it at the back of a display, a slender ring of palest gold with a tiny, glowing pink sapphire in its own box.

"Come on," said Charlie, heading for the door.

"You can't. You don't even know how much it is."

"Then let's go and ask."

She rang the bell and after being scrutinised through the glass of the door, they were let in by an elderly dapper man in a dark blue suit with a matching batwing polka dot bow tie.

"The pink…"

"Sapphire, my dear? On the middle shelf?"

Charlie nodded, ignoring the tugging at her sleeve and then the hissing in her ear.

The shop was small and the shop owner must have heard Miranda's protestations, but he retrieved the ring from the display and took it to the counter where he placed it on a small, flat cushion of black velvet beneath a lamp. Miranda gasped. It was even more beautiful there than it had appeared through the shop window.

"A small pink sapphire set in eighteen karat rose gold, hall-marked London, 1918."

"Can she try it on?" asked Charlie.

"Of course. I suspect it was meant as an engagement ring," he added as Charlie lifted the ring and slipped it onto the tip the middle finger of Miranda's right hand.

"Too small," said Miranda. She was disappointed and relieved at the same time.

"That shouldn't be a problem," said the man. "Jerome?"

From some shadowy corner a much younger man appeared. He was in his shirt sleeves and wearing an apron. As he squeezed in behind the counter, smiling, the older man produced a set of measuring rings. He soon assessed the size of Miranda's finger and Jerome looked at the ring. He nodded. "I could stretch that, miss," he said. "It's only a size up."

"Or there's a very similar ring with a blue sapphire," said the older man, reaching beneath the glass top and pulling out a tray of rings. He extracted one and placed it on the black cushion.

Charlie was mesmerised, forgot to breathe. The tiny blue sapphire twisted the universe, engulfed her.

"How much?" she managed to ask.

"Which one?"

"Both."

"Charlie!"

Charlie turned to look at Miranda. Whatever else Miranda had been about to say died on her lips. She was overwhelmed. Mostly by love, but also by some other intensity she could not put a name to.

The older man cleared his throat. "Sixty pounds for both and that includes resizing."

As Charlie pulled her cheque book out from an inner pocket, Miranda had to turn away to hide her tears.

No One But You

It hadn't been a long argument or particularly heated. Miranda had told Charlie off for being so extravagant with the money her Nan had left her, for being so impulsive. Charlie had said she sounded just like Daisy. They had agreed that wasn't a bad thing, and tired out by their day they had eaten, bathed, and gone to bed.

"Are you awake," whispered Miranda to the darkness.

A hand sought out hers beneath the sheets.

"I love you."

The hand griped tighter and there was rustling of bedclothes as Charlie rolled onto her side. There had been such passion in those simple words. She engulfed Miranda in her embrace. "Forever," she whispered in her ear. "With all my heart."

My Midnight Pillow

Close The Door

In serried ranks the fallen were stacked in every direction as far as the eye could see, as high as the corrugated roof would allow. Mostly anonymous, some were inscribed on their sides with cryptic chalk marks in different colours. She walked slowly through the drying sheds, passing great oak balks destined to be beams and joists, broad planks marked out for floors, other lengths and thicknesses destined for furniture workshops. With an almost idle curiosity, she touched the lengths of seasoning timber. Rough surfaces scratched at her fingertips.

Wandering into another aisle she let her fingers drag lightly along some fresh cut pine still being stacked, picking up a tacky residue of resin. Bringing her fingertips to her face she inhaled the clean, pine odour, reminded of Em's parents' hoopla stall.

She smiled, unconsciously reaching to feel the sapphire ring on its chain beneath her shirt.

"Hello, Miss Cornelius."

Charlie turned with a smile. "Mr Edwards."

"What can we do for Simmons' today?"

"Mahogany," said Charlie and handed over a piece of paper with a sketch and measurements.

"What's this, then?" asked Mr Edwards, pulling his glasses out of the top pocket of his brown work coat.

"Frame for a mirror."

"Oh. She found it then?"

"No," sighed Charlie. "Still looking. But I thought I'd put some timber by. Work on the carvings."

"For a surprise, like?"

"Maybe. Not sure I'll be able to keep it hidden, but that's the idea."

"Won't hear about it from us."

"And I'll pay out of my own pocket to keep the books straight."

They took their time, pulling lengths off the stacks of well seasoned timber, turning each piece to look for knots, to test if it was true, examining the grain. In the end, they carried three lengths into the cutting shed where one of the apprentices marked up the timber under the watchful eye of Mr Edwards before manoeuvring each piece onto the circular saw table.

With a biting whine and spray a deep red dust, the mahogany was cut to nine foot lengths. Charlie watched fascinated as the apprentice worked with such calmness close to the deadly blade.

"No more dangerous than riding bikes up a wall, I shouldn't wonder," said Mr Edwards with a grin when it was quiet.

"Each to their own," replied Charlie lifting one of the cut pieces.

The van was parked out on the street and she lifted the timber piece by piece and slid it carefully into the rear. As she was loading the fifth and final piece, a train whistle from the nearby station made her glance up and along the street.

In the distance was the railway station with its square tower and canopy. Deep in conversation, three figures were mounting the steps to the booking hall. One of the men seemed to be wearing a military uniform, the other was whey-faced and thin, swamped by the heavy coat he wore. Between them, a young woman. A cold shiver worked its way through Charlie's body.

Mr Edwards, who had come out with the receipt for Charlie's payment, found an abandoned van, doors wide open. Bemused, he looked round and caught a glimpse of Charlie as she pushed her way through the entrance doors of the railway station. He closed up the van and waited.

On the station platform Charlie stood watching the rear of the train as it pulled past the signals and away, leaving great curls of steam and smoke in its wake.

"No. No," she said to herself, unable to look away. "I don't want to travel. Not now."

"You're in the wrong place, then," said a passing porter, overhearing her plea.

Charlie blinked herself back into the here and now.

"Is it Waterloo you're wanting?" asked the porter. "Next one won't be too long."

Charlie stood for a moment, bemused. "What? No. Sorry. I thought I saw some… No. It's all right. Thank you."

She wandered out through the ticket office and down the steps, the porter shaking his head as he watched her go.

On the pavement, with the world wending its way about her, she stood oblivious, cut off by a strange braiding of elation and fear, of misery and longing, of conflicting desires. She had promised Miranda, once, that if ever she stepped sideways again she would take her along. But there, in the dusty March sunshine, she knew the only travelling she wanted right now was here, with the fair, where Miranda was safe.

Her hand wandered once more to the ring where it hung beneath her shirt, aware of the paradox – the sapphire was the doorway and it was also now the anchor.

Give Me Your Word

"It was so romantic," said Lorna. "One moment he's standing under the awning peering out at the rain and says: 'Another bloody summer, pissing it down.'" They listened a moment to the rain drumming on the roof of their van. "Then he turns to me and says: 'Do you want to get married?'"

"Well he certainly knows how to win over a woman," said Charlie.

Lorna snorted.

"What?"

"Go on, Beetle, tell 'em what you did."

Beth grinned. "I merely took my brother off to one side and told him if he ever hurt Lorna they would never find his body."

It was Mary's turn to snort. "When did he ever listen to us?"

"I threatened him with Charlie."

"What?!"

"Harry used to be well leery of you. Remember when you first turned up in our shelter with Alice?"

"I thought he just didn't like me."

"He thought you were a ghost or something."

Charlie risked a quick glance at Miranda who stared back wide-eyed.

When the rainstorm had passed, thunder still grumbling away in the distance, Charlie went with Miranda to check that the Mirror sideshow was ready for opening before moving on to the Wall.

"It's not fair," said Miranda as they stood in the dark with the mirrors.

Charlie did not need to ask.

Lorna and Harry engaged, with announcements, and a fair-ground wedding in the offing. Charlie held her close.

"Do you think there'll ever be a time we can…? I don't know... get married," said Miranda. "Just be us without fear of…"

Charlie held her tighter.

"Who knows," she finally replied. "The world is a strange place. Maybe one day we'll even have kids."

Miranda grimaced and Charlie laughed.

Blue Star

"Can't make its mind up," said Beth about the weather when Charlie joined her under the awning. She accepted the bottle of pop, pulled from a bucket filled with half-melted ice.

In front of them the last of the audience from the final show of the night made their way down the steep steps that curved down the outside of Old Tom, chattering loudly. Even though it was late evening, it was still hot and the inside of the Wall would be thick with exhaust fumes and slick with condensation from their final performance.

Mary joined them. "Harry and Lorna are sorting the bikes." They all sniggered, knowing the two of them wanted to be left alone for a bit. "I reckon we should take the roof off," she added as she sat and helped herself to a bottle from the bucket.

"That'll make it rain," said Beth.

"We could do with some," replied Mary, "but I reckon this'll last."

"Maybe fold a panel back," said Charlie watching the crowds thin as lights began to go out on some of the larger rides. "That should be enough. I'll go up in the morning—"

"No you won't," said Mary, "not if you're on watch tonight. Do your stint and have a lie in. We'll sort it."

Charlie gave in. When the drinks were finished and Lorna and Harry had been prised out of the ride, they locked up. The princesses headed back to their van and Charlie ambled across the site to help Miranda close up the mirrors and haul her takings round to their own little van.

After a hurried supper, Charlie left Miranda curled up with one of her old Arthur Ransome books and did her rounds. She said goodnight to those still closing up or doing last minute maintenance in the relative cool of the night and then checked all the shadows and nooks for lurkers and courting couples oblivious to the time.

Strange Lady In Town

Midnight came and went. One o'clock. All the rides were dark. Most of the living vans were dark as well, one or two with open doors and folk little more than dark shadows sitting out on their steps. The gaudy nomadic village was silent in the hot scented dark.

The funfair dreamed. Long after the last punter had traipsed home eating chips or hugging the bear they had won, long after the last sideshow operator had washed up their supper things and crawled into bed, long after the street lights had flickered off and shop displays had gone dark, the funfair drifted into sleep with all its memories of the day playing out.

In its nocturnal reveries, small children squeal and run about clutching handfuls of long-saved pennies and threepenny bits in their pockets; teenagers laugh and giggle and pose, playing out the endless games that establish a pecking order; mating rituals are started, cemented, or brought crashing to a tear-stained end; adults remember their youth, capturing it vicariously through the excitement of their children or snatching brief moments of their own. All against a gaudy background of flashing lights, loud music, whirling rides, enticing aromas, bright paintings, and exotic cries from the barkers.

The funfair dreams of the other side as well, of the world behind the bright canvas and board, of the machinery and wires, of the blood and sweat, of the tears and laughter, of the sheer hard work involved in smiling in the face of complaints and anger, of the relief in taking joy in the joy of others.

Charlie felt it all as she wandered about the site in the dark, her own chimera fluttering after her like an ethereal cloak, the frayed edges tangling with the dreams of the fair. Of all the things about the fair she loved, this she loved second best.

With a loving smile she stopped at the foot of the steps up to Miranda's mirrors. The faintest rumble of thunder growled its way across the summer sky like a discontented cat. From the top of the steps she was able to see across most of the fair. As with each other patrol, it was quiet. The key from her pocket unlocked the door and she slipped inside.

Inside, the dreams were stranger, muted, elusive, as if they had somewhere to hide, somewhere to escape. Although there was no light inside the van, she knew exactly where each mirror was, moved quietly between them, touching each carved frame as she passed. When she reached the centre, the place where you turned and saw the plain mirror after all the distortions, she stopped.

All around her the mirrors stood and she felt as if they were waiting, patiently. They shimmered, distorting the dark like a heat haze in a way that hurt her eyes. She knew she could see nothing, knew there was nothing to see, yet something within the mirrors yearned to be acknowledged. They opened darkness onto darkness, doorways through which to explore, doorways through which to become lost, doorways filled with a dancing infinite nothing, doorways filled stars, doorways like deep and icy drowning pools.

Trodden down parched grass in a pool of torchlight calmed her as she sat and wondered if anyone had heard her slam the door before locking it with shaking hands. Dreams. Too many dreams.

On her second round, after climbing down from the roof of Old Tom, she became aware of being watched. Ignored it and continued to check that everywhere was secure. As she returned to the Wall, she saw the figure sitting on the steps to the payment booth. Tall, slim, a heart-shaped face beneath an old-fashioned page-boy haircut. Beside her was a neatly folded coat.

"Hello, Charlie."

Charlie stopped in front of the woman. "Alone?"

A smile and a nod. "I'm Una. Join me?"

"I think I'm happy here, thank you."

"Danse d'abord; pense plus tard," said the woman softly.

"Dancing? Is that what you call it?"

A wave of misery swept over Charlie, threatened to pull her away from the shore where she had found warmth and shelter.

"I *have* danced," she continued. "When I was supposed to be playing. I'm done with it now."

"Yet still you wear a sapphire," said Una.

Charlie touched the front of her shirt, feeling the warm hardness of the ring. "It's a bond to the ones I love. And a reminder of the grief it brought to some."

Una gasped. "You remember that?"

"Not clearly, but when your mother is that upset, it rocks the foundation of your world. That's not something that's easy to forget. Like seeing a pair of blue shoes…" She couldn't finish.

Una sighed and patted the empty step beside her. "That's all I meant."

Charlie looked at the worn planking for a moment and then sat herself beside Una, studying her unashamedly in the faint light. She nearly asked her other name but wasn't sure she wanted to get that involved. Not any more.

"There's nothing you could have done," Una said. "And I know you tried."

"I thought *you* were my mother. When I first saw you," said Charlie, not convinced and not wanting, in any case, to talk of old failures and painful losses.

A slight frown crossed the pale face. “Remind me. It’s not always easy to keep track.”

It was Charlie’s turn to frown. “1940. The shelter. The school.”

Una stared into the dark for a moment and then nodded.

“You don’t seem to have aged,” added Charlie. “And those other times. Later. I knew you couldn’t be her. When I saw you clearly for the first time. I remember her. Just. Besides. She wouldn’t turn up. Not now. Not after all this time.”

Una looked like she wanted to explain yet it was clear she didn’t know where to begin, didn’t even know if there was a beginning. Or an end. “She loves you,” was all she could manage in the end. “And one day, I hope, you’ll see for yourself. But you’re right. Now is not the time for you to dance. You have the keys. The doors can always be opened.”

“What’s the point of it if you can’t go back and change things?” asked Charlie.

“The point? There is no point, no narrative to be retold, no shape to be remoulded. It is chaos and we are… dancers.”

“So you never try to change anything?”

Una laughed softly and sadly. “All the time, Charlie. All the time. That’s our tragedy.”

Una stood and turned to face Charlie, reaching down to pick up her greatcoat. Charlie shook her head. “I’ve learned a new dance,” she said. “One with a happy ending.”

“I envy you. All this.” She lifted an arm to take in the fairground. “Hold on tight.”

Of a sudden, she looked tired and very much older. Sweeping round and settling her coat on her shoulders, she strode away, fading into the shadows of unasked questions and landscapes that were not there.

All That Calm Sunday

A Woman In Love

The bandage on her left hand was grubby after the day's work so she kept it as hidden as she could in the folds of her jacket. She would have worn gloves, but they were too tight and that made the wound throb. Besides, it's not easy to look at books with gloves on. All because of a stupid argument that had flared up out of nowhere.

The princesses had found a workshop space for Charlie to carve the new mirror frame in secret. They had called it a workshop. Charlie thought of it as the lean-to, some bits of roofing tin nailed together round a bench and propped up against the back of one of the sheds on the site at Leatherhead.

It had taken Miranda just three days to find it.

"It was meant to be a secret," Charlie had complained.

Miranda had found herself a stool and a cushion and installed them in the darkest corner where she could sit and watch. Charlie had carried on practising with the wood carving chisels she had found in a second hand shop. It was her belief that Miranda would soon get cold and bored. Which only goes to prove, she thought to herself as she took another book from the shelf, just how little she had reckoned on Miranda's stubborn streak.

She put the book back and wandered toward another part of the shop, glancing toward the counter to see if the owner had reappeared. He hadn't. She continued browsing, but her mind was on other things, especially when she rested the book in the crook of the thumb and forefinger of her left hand. With a grimace, she removed it and put it back on the shelf, not realising it was upside down.

It was the constant presence that got to her in the end. She loved Miranda dearly, loved her with a passion that sometimes frightened her, but having her sit silently watching every move she made... It was bound to end in blood or tears, she thought.

And was grateful it was her own blood, grateful it was just in the fleshy part of the finger where it had been easy to stitch up.

It began to dawn on her that someone had called her name. She turned to see the owner at the counter, his hand resting lightly on a book.

"You got it?" she asked. "That's excellent."

"Shall I wrap it?"

"Yes please."

Charlie watched, her sombre mood gone. This was one secret she would definitely be able to keep, one surprise she could spring unspoiled. A beautiful edition of *Alice's Adventures in Wonderland and Through the Looking Glass* as illustrated by Mervyn Peake. It was mostly for Miranda, but also for Charlie herself, not least because Peake's Alice reminded her of Miranda as she had been when they first met.

"Twelve and six, please."

Charlie dug out a ten shilling note from her wallet and a half crown from the change in her pocket and placed them on the counter. "Thank you," she said as she left.

Pleased with herself at the sumptuous volume, she hesitated for a moment. Was it the right thing? Was it not more for herself and her memories? But it was only a moment and she shrugged her doubts away. Miranda loved the stories and the illustrations were truly wonderful and, anyway, why should she not share this memory, this pleasure, with the one she loved?

Two Different Worlds

"Nobody's interested in a bar of chocolate as a prize any more. I mean. A prize is a prize, ain't it? Never understood 'em. Punters. No problem sellin' 'em candy floss since sugar came off rationing, but their faces when they win a bar of this." He held up a bar of Cadbury's Dairy Milk. "That's a bob's worth, that is, and they look like they've just had their arses smacked. I got boxes of 'em."

"We've got some old cigarette machines somewhere. I could probably rejig one to take shilling pieces, drop a bar into the drawer. People still like buying from machines."

Paul grunted, tidying the rifle left by the last punter. "They was good for basic prizes. Small. Long lasting. Easy to store. I won't have goldfish. Cruel that is. Could have ciggies for adults, but I still need something for the kiddies."

"I'll give it some thought," said Charlie as she picked up a rifle and broke the barrel to prime it, feeding in a pellet from her private supply.

"Bloody glad you ain't a punter. I'd have no prizes left," he said as metal ducks started to go down with a metallic tink. Charlie smiled to herself, glad of the tip John had given her years ago to find something to calm herself after an evening on the bikes on the Wall. Five minutes knocking down tin targets did wonders and she was always relaxed by the time she got to Miranda to help close up the mirrors.

After they had washed up the supper things, Charlie spent ten minutes looking at the mechanism from a cigarette machine but was soon distracted and abandoned the pieces on the small table. They talked for a while afterwards, small, warm, sleepy voices whispering in the narrow, enfolding space.

She stood for a long time in the brilliant dark staring down at the broken surface of the deep pool as it froze over once more. Ghosts kept vigil with her, shimmering on the edge of vision, each as cold as the deep winter night. There was no perceptible change as she waited and watched. The black surface of the pool with its fragments of floating ice was now still, freezing, drowning the man and sealing the corpse away from the world.

When she was finally able to tear away from the freezing grasp of the dark, shattered ice, she looked up to see it was snowing. Great flakes floating out of a windless sky, wisping down through darkness visible to obscure the surroundings. Torn and broken buildings wavered in the white world, fading, dancing, transforming, a playground full of silent ghosts running across the ground in front of her. For one anxious moment she worried they might fall into… but there was nothing to fall into, just a bright patch of scuffed grass between the big rides.

It was the first time she had seen the fair in the snow, bright flakes layering everything with light. She ran whirling through the snowfall, feeling the light fill her, knowing she had to share it. Breathless, she fetched up against the steps of the gallopers, climbed them to see if she could spot Miranda. Only then did it come home to her that she was alone and the fairground was still and deserted, like a tiny model in a snow globe, like a mechanical diorama.

Lights flashed in the distance and she held her breath. Where was Miranda? Where was… Vague shapes in the distance and she was breathing again. Clattering and thundering, a sudden desire to be gone, running past the dodgem cars where they lay neglected and rusty. How did that happen so quickly? And the big wheel with yellow cars? Looming above her in the snow and the growing darkness.

She retreated, found herself running between sideshows and living vans, calling out for Miranda with a voice that even she could not hear.

"I'm here."

Charlie woke to the warmth of her bed and the sound of Miranda soothing her.

"Just a dream."

She reached out and enveloped Miranda, held her close trying to quell the fear induced by that looming Ferris wheel.

Rip It Up

Gathered in a circle and wearing their traditional garb of many layers – scarves, balaclavas, woolly hats and heavy boots, they stood for a moment in silence. Heat rose from the paraffin stove, creating a small column of warmth in the warehouse. They had clustered round it to warm their hands through their mittens, waiting for the tin mugs of tea that Charlie had just poured for them. Strong tea dosed from the can of condensed milk.

Outside, snow had been falling in passing showers. Silent and cold. The late November sky was low and grey. Much like the mood indoors. They had been hard at work all morning stripping down the gallopers and laying all the components out on large tarpaulins. There was a long, cold afternoon's work ahead of them.

John was responsible for the wooden horses, their repair and repainting. He had a large lever arch file in which he had compiled information on each one, its position, name, diagrams to show colours, repairs made, and so on. Just like Miranda had done on a smaller scale with her mirrors. The others were there to check the structure was still sound, overhaul the machinery, and hand over the delicate mechanism of the organ to Charlie. When they finally extracted it.

In the meantime, she brewed tea, ferried sandwiches from the house, and fretted about Miranda who was moping about ever since a promising lead from a Sunderland glass factory had turned out to be a dead end.

As she was gathering the empty mugs a deep thud made the floor tremble and everyone stopped what they were doing and looked up. Even now, years later, there were heart pounding moments of apprehension and flickering memories when they were caught unawares.

Charlie was first to the street door and peered out. Thin snow drifted past. Down the hill, the road was empty. Someone nudged Charlie and she turned her head in the other direction. A transporter with a heavy crane stood at the top of the hill and another thump shuddered through the ground as the second loading ramp was dropped.

With nothing to do in the warehouse, Charlie left the others to go back to dismantling the roundabout. As she closed the door she could hear them raise their voices in chorus: "There's a song that I recall, My mother sang to me…"

Tall enough now to wear the old greatcoat comfortably over the Guthrie, she walked up the icy pavement with an easy grace born of strength and confidence, a faint smile on her face. She passed the derelict stables and the small furniture repair workshop that never seemed to be open, stopped a moment at the side wall of the back yard of the corner shop to make sure it was safe, and then crossed the road to where two workmen stood.

Beyond the transporter was another lorry from which a watchman's shed was being manhandled. Charlie waited while the two men finished their discussion of how best to decant the crane, looking at the scarred metal wrecking ball where it swayed slightly against its tether, looking at the faded name painted along the side.

"Yes, miss?"

"The old houses coming down?"

"That's it. We've to clear the whole row. Building new ones in the New Year when the weather gets better. Flats, they'll be. Two storey. You interested?"

She hadn't even thought of it. "It's just we're doing some work in the warehouse, painting, delicate stuff."

He looked downhill to where she was pointing. Back to the houses. "Shouldn't be more than a couple of weeks," he said. "P'raps less. Shoddy state them houses."

Charlie shrugged. There was not much they could do except work round it. "OK. Thanks."

She left them to it and walked back down to the warehouse door. More snow was falling and it was getting darker. She was surrounded by grim brick walls and decay, plagued by memories of the Blitz and the ghosts that had haunted the ruins, of the things she had seen and done as a child, of a fear she could not shake that one day, the past would reach out and grab her ankle and, despite all that anchored her to the here and now, would pull her slowly away from this warm future she had found.

The moment of horror passed and she pushed herself away from the wall against which she had staggered. Before she let herself back into the relative warmth, she stopped and gazed across at the forsaken row of dead houses, pulled out her notebook and, in defiance of the past, she wrote down the builder's name.

The Ninth Anneal

Silhouettes

"Is this right?" asked Charlie as she rested her helmet on the handlebars.

It looked like a terrace of grimy stone-built houses, lining one side of a short cobbled street. Charlie's heart missed a beat, they looked tiny to her adult eye, but replace the stone with brick and it could have been her Nan's house, her Nan's street. A small, lost child danced in a dream.

Miranda reached over Charlie's shoulder and waved a piece of paper. She took the hint and turned off the engine. Opposite, a dairy filled the air with the brittle sound of thousands of empty bottles rattling along a conveyor, equally empty floats were parked in a line beneath the awning of a loading bay.

With the thrum of the motor gone they were able to pick out other sounds they couldn't identify.

Charlie felt Miranda climb off the pillion, dropped the stand and, leaving her helmet on the handlebars, climbed off herself.

A door opened in the dairy and a man in a brown work coat came out. He fished in his pocket and produced a pipe. As he was stuffing the bowl from a pouch, Miranda approached. He looked up.

"Yes, lass?"

"Is that the glass factory?"

The man laughed. "Aye. Looks like breeze has blown door shut. Just walk in." He pointed to a door of one of the houses directly opposite. "Office is just inside."

"Bike all right just here?" asked Charlie.

"Aye. She'll be fine."

They both said thanks and crossed to the opposite pavement. Miranda hesitated in the doorway. It had been a long search with many disappointments. Charlie heard her take a deep breath, wanted to hug her.

"I'm here," she said.

Miranda nodded and pushed forward.

"Prop it open," someone called. "Thanks."

Charlie looked down and saw an old, wooden wedge, dark and greasy with age. She kicked it under the door and followed Miranda into a small office that must once have been a parlour. The hearth in the fireplace was laid ready for lighting. The mantelpiece was lined with various awards. A calendar hung on the chimney breast above them. Elsewhere filling cabinets lined the wall and a small desk in the window was currently unoccupied apart from piles of paper.

The room was dominated by a larger desk and by the middle aged woman who sat behind it. She looked up from a type-writer. The hint of a frown crossed her face when she saw Miranda and Charlie in their black leathers. Miranda smiled. It could melt glaciers, that smile, as Charlie knew only too well.

"I wrote," said Miranda. "My name is Russ. About the fairground mirror."

They were used to watching people's faces as they made the adjustment. Fairground people. Women. In bike leathers.

"Russ?" She lifted a buff folder from the desk beside her and opened it, scanning the top letter before looking at Miranda again.

Charlie could see Miranda's neat typing on the Simmons headed notepaper, her formal signature at the bottom of the page – M Russ.

"Miranda Russ."

Charlie glowed with pride at the steel edge in Miranda's quiet voice. She wanted to grab her and kiss her and had to stop her-self from giggling.

"Yes," said the woman. "Sorry. Excuse me a moment, I'll go and find Mr Robertson."

The second she was out of the room, Charlie stepped up behind Miranda, placed her hands on her shoulders and kissed the back of her head.

"Stop it," whispered Miranda, but she reached up and squeezed one of Charlie's hands.

By the time the secretary returned with Mr Robertson they were standing side by side staring innocently at the wall like pupils waiting in a head teacher's office, not something Miranda had ever experienced. They turned to face him as he came in

"Sorry to have kept you waiting, lass," said Mr Robertson looking from one to the other.

Miranda put out her hand and he shook it.

"Miranda Russ. And my associate, Charlotte Cornelius."

"The mirror."

Miranda nodded.

"Well, I'm not sure how you got on to us," he said.

Charlie could sense Miranda sag. No one else would have noticed the minute change, but she knew.

"We've not done that sort of work. Not in my time, anyway. I had to go ask my Dad. He's retired now, but he said when he were younger, he remembers his Dad taking on a special job."

The sag was still there, Miranda refusing to get her hopes up.

"Spent days going through all the old paperwork did Mrs Smithson." He nodded at the secretary. They turned. She held up an old box file, passed it to Mr Robertson. He perched it on the paperwork on the unoccupied desk and opened it up, flakes of desiccated sellotape dropping to the floor.

From within he removed copies of letters and receipts which he handed to Miranda. Charlie could almost hear the squeal as she took them and devoured the contents.

"Great great grandma Elizabeth, Alice's mum," said Miranda breathless with excitement, passing a letter to Charlie. "That's her original order."

As Charlie was reading it, a detailed order for twenty-seven mirrors according to enclosed specifications, Miranda handed her the receipts.

"Sorry to dampen things," said Charlie, "but I got the impression you don't do this sort of thing any more."

She hated to do it, but she didn't want Miranda getting her hopes up.

"That's right. Just flat mirrors these days. Mostly domestic, although we do make larger ones for shops and the like. Curved glass is a special trick. And you'd need the pattern if you was to replace the original you've lost."

“Stop teasing the lass,” said Mrs Smithson from behind her typewriter.

Heads turned sharply.

Mrs Smithson looked over her glasses at Miranda. “There’s more in that box.”

Heads turned back.

An unapologetic Mr Robertson lifted a book out of the box. “The original pattern book and,” with an extra flourish a stage magician would have been proud of, “the original drawings.”

Miranda stared at the sheaf of folded papers, hardly daring to ask. “Does that mean…?”

Mr Robertson’s grinned fit to split. “You tell us which one and we’ll have a good go.”

This time Miranda did squeal. And when she remembered she was a woman of twenty-five, she stepped across the office to Mrs Smithson. “Thank you so much for finding the letters and things. It’s been a long search.”

Something that may have been a smile moved the secretary’s features. “Go on with you,” she said flapping a hand. “Sid’ll want to show you the factory.”

With a grin verging on tearfulness, Miranda turned to Charlie. “Go on, follow the man,” Charlie said and watched as Miranda went out into the hallway. She turned to the secretary. “I’d like to say thank you as well. She’s been looking for that missing mirror for years.”

“Tell your friend to call back in here before you leave. Sid had the drawing office make copies of the pattern book and the big patterns. She can take the originals with her.”

Charlie nodded. “Don’t be surprised if she tries to give you a hug.”

“Get away with you.”

Stepping out into the hallway, Charlie saw the back of Miranda as she went through a doorway. She ran out to the bike and retrieved her Brownie Cresta from one of the panniers, running back in. She caught up with the others and found herself in a kitchen where they waited for her. More memories assailed her.

She pushed them aside. Nothing was going to spoil Miranda's day or her appreciation of it.

What had once been the back door of the house let them through from a domestic world of old tea mugs and a giant brown teapot lined up on an old deal table into a species of hell populated by demons who clocked on at eight and off at five, one o'clock on Saturdays.

The noise they had been conscious of rushed at them as the heavy connecting door was opened. So too did the heat and the scent of scorched sand.

It was an industrial cavern of shadow and fitful light, cast iron pillars supporting a soot caked roof. On the far side, furnaces roared and cast their orange glow. Charlie undid her jacket, saw Miranda do the same.

Attending the altars of fire with long metal rods in a well-practised ritual, eight men in long leather aprons, heads protected with flat caps, moved back and forth across the floor, weaving light as they went. Lustrous orbs of luminous glass danced in the apparent gloom, their incandescence fading as they were spun and shaped, taken back to the heat. The faces of the men seemed cadaverous, lit from beneath by the sunset glow of the pliable glass. Charlie took several pictures not knowing whether they would come out.

Oblivious of their audience, the serious faced men moved non stop with care, immersed in the noise of the furnaces and the sound of glass, shouts cutting through the din. One passed close by with a long wooden tray of bowls balanced on his head. They watched in awe as he reached up and with deft movements removed the board and slotted it onto a rack. Not one of the glass bowls moved.

"I reckon people'd pay to see that at the fair," said Charlie.

Miranda nodded. The man turned and gave them both a broad toothless grin and cheery wink before returning calmly to his elemental work.

"We make all sorts now," said Sid Robertson, his voice penetrating the clamour without effort.

"They'd make great top swag. Star Prizes. At the fair."

"Don't worry," grinned Sid. "You'll not be going away without a catalogue."

He beckoned and they followed, picking their way along a path that ran across one corner of the shed to another set of doors.

The second shed was marginally quieter than the first. More furnaces roared, but the work was slower, large sheets of glass moving along roller conveyers, poked and turned, sliced and shaped, slid onto trolleys that were hauled back to a furnace to begin the journey again.

"This is the shop where we'll do it." Sid pointed to a section away from the furnaces where mounds of fine sand covered the floor. Charlie took more photographs before they followed Sid over to a quieter corner. "We'll mould the shape of the glass from the pattern using that sand and clay mix. Then we lay a sheet of hot glass over it and work it into the mould."

"Bet that's not as simple as it sounds," said Miranda.

Sid laughed. "More than I could manage. Albert, the chap over there," he pointed to a skinny man who looked like he'd be far better holding up beans in the garden, "he's the artist."

They watched Albert trimming strips of molten glass from a plate, creating a scalloped edge. The waste was dropped into a bucket and taken away by a youth who wandered through to the other workshop, returning shortly after to pick up more trimmings. It was all fascinating, but nothing could match the happiness in Miranda's face and the joy Charlie took in seeing it there.

Rip It Up

At that time of the evening, the A65 was quiet. Rush hour was over. Just a few long-haul lorries were parked outside the café. They pushed in through the door and along the aisle between the Formica topped tables with their fixed benches. It was warm and bright, relatively quiet. The lorry drivers sat at their tables, eating as they read their evening papers. Behind the counter, a pale girl watched them approach. Her eyes had lit up for a brief moment when they first came in. Perhaps it was the leathers they wore. As soon as she realised they were strangers, however, her interest faded.

The yellowed dial of an old radio perched on the counter glowed with a faint light. As they approached, a serious voice informed them: "Russia has launched a satellite into space. It is the first man-made object to leave the Earth's atmosphere. TASS, the Russian news agency, said the satellite, named *Sputnik*, was 560 miles above the Earth and orbiting the globe every ninety minutes.

"Scientists say the metal sphere will eventually return to Earth, burning up in the atmosphere. Both Russia and the United States of America have programmes to launch more satellites in the hope they will provide—"

A face peered through the plastic fly curtain from the kitchen, a man in need of a shave. He lifted his chin in a half nod, turned down the radio with a muttered, "As if we didn't have enough to worry about," and disappeared again. Miranda chose a seat and Charlie ordered. She knew what they both liked.

As Charlie sat, facing the counter, a heavy lorry roared past outside, rattling the steamy windows. She looked at Miranda across the table whose eyes were still alive with the joy of finally having found someone who could replace the missing mirror.

"You'll wear that away before we get home, if you keep doing that."

Miranda's hand shot away from the zippered pocket that contained the wallet with the documents from the glass factory.

"Will not," she said.

Charlie made sure no one could see her face and then poked out the tip of her tongue.

"Talking of home," said Miranda, ignoring the provocation, "where are we? I don't remember passing this on the way up."

"Oh well," replied Charlie, her face serious. "Now's as good as any time to tell you."

"Tell me what?"

"We're not going home."

"What? Why?"

"I thought we'd run away and join a circus."

"Very funny. What's going on? We have to get back to move the lorries."

"All arranged."

"What? When did you do that? Who is moving them?"

"Mary and Beth, with a bit of help from the Cutwood boys. I sorted it when you heard from Robertsons."

"But why? What's happening? I thought we were going straight back. I haven't packed anything."

"All done."

"So where are we going?"

Charlie didn't answer. The girl from behind the counter arrived with a tray and decanted two plates of egg and chips, a plate of bread and butter, and two mugs of tea.

"Cutlery's over there," she said as she turned away.

Miranda scooted out of her bench seat and crossed to the small table on the other side, returning straight away with the utensils she had picked from the wooden tray.

"Well?" she asked as she sat down again.

Charlie picked up a chip and popped it her mouth. "Can't talk with my mouth full," she said.

Miranda kicked her shin.

"Tell, or I'll confiscate that," she said, pointing at Charlie's plate with a fork.

"It's a surprise holiday. We've got a week to ourselves."

"But will we get there tonight? Won't you be too tired?"

"It's not too far and I had a decent break while you were sorting out all the details at the factory. Never seen so much paperwork."

Miranda looked at Charlie for a few seconds with narrowed eyes. Charlie ignored her, a faint smile on her lips. It had been a long time in the planning, and everything had depended on Miranda finally locating the factory that could replace the missing mirror. It seemed to her to be the perfect opportunity to disappear for a few days and, away from all the distractions, with Miranda's mind finally at rest, ask the question that had been on her mind these last ten months or so. Miranda turned her attention to her meal, but beneath the table she slipped her feet around Charlie's, almost as if she had read Charlie's mind.

As they were thinking of leaving, Charlie heard the door bang open and saw Miranda's face harden.

"Trouble," she said. "One and three."

Charlie had guessed without turning round that potential trouble had lurched into the café. Miranda had confirmed it. A leader with three followers. Miranda was good at spotting them and picking out the ring leaders. On the fairground the whole community would know by now. Here they were alone. Turning slightly in her seat, she freed her feet and felt the wall at her shoulder.

"That your bike? That Shadow? Wouldn't mind a go on that."

It was a swaggering voice as if the matter was already decided and he was just waiting for someone to hand over the key. Charlie didn't move as he reached their table and leered down at Miranda.

"Wouldn't mind a go on that either."

Someone sniggered.

Charlie watched his face as he turned to her, watched the confusion emerge.

"You're both girls."

Charlie sighed, raising an eyebrow.

"Are you queers? You don't want all that," he said, turning back to Miranda. "What you need is a proper fucking."

There was ice in Miranda's smile. The sort that would make any sensible person back away. A long way away. Before turning and running.

"I'd need a man for that," she said sweetly. "Would you be holding his coat?"

Not walking away had been his first mistake. Charlie watched with interest as the insult filtered through the dense swamp of his thought processes. His second mistake, and his last for a while, was raising his hand to slap Miranda.

As he leaned in, Charlie lifted her legs and swivelled on the bench. With her back square to the wall for leverage, she kicked out hard. Her boots hit the biker's knees with all the strength that years of riding the Wall had given her and knocked his legs out from underneath him. He dropped face first onto the end of the table and bounced, unconscious before he hit the floor amid a shower of broken crockery.

Charlie was on her feet before anyone could react. No one else moved. With her left hand she reached into a pocket and pulled out a small roll of money, peeled off a couple of five pound notes.

Knowing Miranda would watch her back, she turned to the café owner who was now standing just in front of his counter holding a well-worn pickaxe handle.

"This," said Charlie, "is for the damage."

The man looked at her, the length of timber swinging easily in his hand. He shook his head. "I reckon you've done me a favour. That little bastard and his gang've been a sodding pain for months," he said, his voice low enough so that no one else could hear. "But do yourself one now and get a long way from here and stay away."

Charlie put the money on the counter anyway and strode down the length of the café with Miranda just in front of her. The other three bikers saw her face and swayed out of their way, one of them falling back against one of the truck drivers. As they stepped out into the cool evening air they could hear shouting and more crockery coming apart.

The Girl Can't Help It

The room was warm and cosy, with room to walk around without twisting to avoid one another. Luxury compared with their usual quarters. Fitted carpet. Twin beds. Their own bathroom. Miranda stood in the doorway staring at it as Charlie locked the door on the world.

"Em?"

She turned, unzipping her jacket.

"Sorry about the café. I know you don't like violence. It's just—"

Miranda had stepped across the room. The tip of her finger on Charlie's lips stopped her mid sentence. When Charlie was silent, Miranda took the finger away and leaned close. The kiss was long and said all that needed to be said in a way words could never convey. Charlie relaxed.

It was midnight when they finished unpacking. They shared a bath, climbed into one bed where they made love, climbed into the other where they slept entwined.

Butterfly

"Are you all right?"

Charlie had emerged from their private bathroom swathed in a towel to see Miranda standing in her underwear in front of the mirror on the chest of drawers, gently massaging her upper arm.

Twirling a finger, she said: "Let me see."

Like the obedient child she could sometimes be, Miranda turned so her arm was bathed in the morning light from the window.

"It still aches a bit," said Miranda.

With gentle fingers, Charlie inspected the spot where Miranda had received her 'flu jab the week before. They had both had them, on Daisy's insistence, along with everyone else at the fair. Not just for the good of the family, she had said, but for punters as well. And the business. She was putting it on all the fliers that staff were protected and couldn't pass it on.

"You'll live," said Charlie. "Long enough for the second jab next week, at least."

"Thanks for reminding me."

Some magnetism held Charlie's fingertips to Miranda's arm, drew Miranda's arms around Charlie. In the early October sunshine they stood in a silent embrace. It was a luxury rarely afforded them, especially on a Saturday morning. On the road there was hardly the room in their little van and someone was bound to hammer on the door needing help or telling them to shake a leg. In the house there was always the danger of someone barging in.

When they finally emerged into daylight, Coniston greeted them with a fresh, still autumnal embrace that they savoured for a moment before Charlie checked over her bike. Happy with the first chore of the day, they went back through the Inn to set out on the second.

"It looks busier than I'd imagined it would be," said Charlie as they dodged between cars to cross the road. An Austin A30 Countryman passed in front of them, two adults with fixed smiles on tired faces in the front, a pile of gurning children with faces and sticky fingers pressed against the windows in the back.

"Glad our room was quiet."

They passed alongside the churchyard, where they could see John Ruskin's elaborately carved grave stone standing tall in the shadow of a yew tree. A small posy of flowers was a splash of colour at its base.

Despite the number of people out and about in the village, they dawdled. Like the occasional private moment, taking their own time to do something was a luxury to be savoured. Right up to the previous night they had been working to a timetable. By the end of the journey, they had been following the headlamp boring a tunnel into the darkness along winding roads, aware only of monochrome glimpses of forest and hill. Even in their sleep they had been travelling. Now it was time to slow down.

Beyond St Andrew's Church they came to the crossroads and there, as directed, they found Martins Bank, right on the bridge over Church Beck. Once that business was dealt with and they had spending money in their pockets, they went back out into the heady air.

"Well?" asked Charlie looking around. "It's your treat. What do you want to do?"

Miranda looked solemn. "Everything," she said.

"That's a Miranda answer if ever I heard one. How about Windermere? We could take the ferry across the lake. Watch for pirates."

Miranda laughed.

Chances Are

At a slower pace than was normal for Charlie, they followed the road to Hawkshead, where they wandered for a while, before carrying on past Esthwaite Water, through Near Sawrey where they stopped again to take a quick look at Hill Top Farm. They had neither of them grown up with Beatrix Potter books, so they didn't linger. From there it was a short hop over and down to the ferry landing at Far Sawrey.

A large house of dark grey stone and slate stood on the top of the promontory.

"We could get the whole family in that," said Miranda. "And park up the whole of the fair."

Charlie looked up at the house. "Not sure I'd want to drive the Wall down these lanes."

"There is that."

"What is it, anyway?"

Miranda wandered over to a board fixed to the wall by the gates, wandered back. "It's called 'The Ferry House'."

"Original."

"There's something called the Freshwater Biological Association based there."

"Smile!"

"Never mind pointing that thing at my ugly mug. Take some pictures of the lake."

They poked the tips of their tongues out at each other; went and took photographs of each other with the lake in the background.

The landing had been deserted when they arrived with the ferry on the far side, just leaving Windermere. As they stood alongside the bike, watching, they nodded amiably to drivers and riders as other cars and bikes coasted into place behind them. Each time a vehicle arrived and cut its engine, there was that blissful moment of silence when birds could be heard again, the lapping of the waters of the lake, talk, laughter.

Charlie and Miranda looked at each other. They both loved working the fair. Neither would ever think of doing anything else. But to be away from all the mechanical hustle, the constant smell of frying onions and sickly scent of candyfloss, the shouts, the loud music, sirens, and flashing lights. And to experience it together was bliss. Even the fact that she could not hold her loved one's hand in public was not going to spoil Charlie's day.

The long, rusty brown ferry arrived, clattering into position, its narrow black chimney shimmering with heat. Chains rattled and the loading ramp scraped against the road. Vehicles disembarked and Charlie started up the bike, rolling on to the open deck once the handful of cars had been manoeuvred aboard. Miranda followed on foot, admiring the ease with which Charlie guided the bike down the narrow space.

As she stepped up the ramp she could feel the vessel wallow in the waters. She joined Charlie by the bike at the front, close to one of the white Kisby rings. As the ferry pulled out to make the journey back to Windermere, she eyed the lowered ramp on which a car was half perched with some misgivings.

"Water's calm," said Charlie quietly. "We'll be fine."

Around them, chatter could barely be heard above the ferry's engine and the swirl of lake water. Motor boats ploughed the surface; rowing boats crawled along or went in circles. Half way across they cruised past a fourteen foot, lug-rigged sailing dinghy with a white sail. Charlie was glad it wasn't being sailed by two young girls wearing red knitted caps otherwise, she feared, Miranda would have exploded with joy. As it was, she hissed, "Pirates!" as the two adult women waved to the ferry's skipper. Charlie took a picture.

"I know, I know," Miranda added. "It's just a story, but let me dream."

Charlie bumped gently against her and winked. They had shared the magic and innocence of the books as children and she had felt that same jolt of excitement as the dinghy passed. They both watched it out of sight.

In Windermere they found somewhere to park the bike and became tourists, wandering in and out shops where they bought postcards, blocked the pavement, wandered in the roadway, and stared at views. Charlie took some photos of Miranda. Miranda took some of Charlie. They persuaded a hiker to take several of them together.

Tired and hungry, they retired to a café where they consumed large helpings of pie and chips. Afterwards, they found a bench and used each other's backs to rest on to write their postcards. Miranda assured her parents they were having a wonderful time and really did wish, in one way, that they could also be there. Charlie wrote to the Indian Princesses, hoping they were managing to survive without her.

Down by the lakeside they consumed more ice cream than was good for them whilst watching the swans and the boats, both hoping for another glimpse of the pirates.

As the afternoon wore on, the air grew chill; a reminder that summer had gone. They strolled back to the bike and, as they had planned, took the long route back to Coniston.

The sun was down when they pulled into the car park of their Inn. It was full of cars and they had to dismount so Charlie could push the Shadow into a space near the back door, just under the kitchen windows. While she fixed the cover, Miranda sidled into the kitchen to scare up some supper to sneak up to their room.

Water Water

Charlie woke to a canopy of golden leaves. She yawned, pulling her thoughts together, mesmerised by the gentle fluttering.

"Em?"

She rolled to one side to see Miranda sitting with her back to a tree, watching. "Hello sleepy-head."

"What time is it?"

Miranda waved a packet of sandwiches, by way of reply.

"Already? Sorry. I didn't mean to."

"It's all right. I've not long woken up myself. After all the noise last night, we both needed it."

"You'd think we'd be used to it."

Miranda shrugged. "That's the fairground. You know all the noises. That lot last night were like a bunch of over-excited kids with too much pocket money. Up and down the bloody stairs and corridors, slamming doors. Why can't they just close them? And all that talking. Twice as annoying cos you couldn't hear what they were saying."

"Here, before you mangle those sandwiches any more."

Miranda passed the pack over to Charlie who was now sitting up.

"Actually…"

Miranda grinned. "There's a good spot just up by the stone wall, there." She pointed. "Well hidden. No nettles."

Charlie scrambled down off the grassy bank where they had slept and walked up the narrow farm track until she found the spot Miranda had mentioned. A cow watched her over the wall as she squatted. It wandered off, clearly unimpressed.

A quick wash of her hands in the beck on the other side of the track and she was back with Miranda.

They sat side by side in the sunshine eating their Sunday lunch, cheese and pickle sandwiches, while watching the stream as it ran into a small pool. Light sparked off the shifting waters, liquescent scintillae that danced in the shaded space in which they rested. A blue lightning flash made them both gasp as a kingfisher dived from its perch.

Charlie felt suddenly tired, disoriented, puzzled by the white cotton dress that covered her legs. Sapphire blue images of a houseboat. The barking of langurs. Birds taking flight. The rattling of a window shutter. A child.

Fingertips brushed her arm. She drew in a deep breath. Miranda did not ask. She had long since grown used to it and knew that Charlie was back.

"Sorry," said Charlie. "The houseboat…"

They had seen an old houseboat that morning, anchored in a bay. It was clearly in need of repair, although it looked as if someone still lived in it. Miranda was delighted; convinced it was Captain Flint's houseboat. Charlie had tried to share the excitement, but too many memories flooded back from her long lost childhood, the houseboats on the lake, the mountains…

That night, amidst all the late night noise, Miranda held Charlie tight and soothed her to sleep. Too restless for sleep herself, she sat with a torch at the tiny writing table and went over all the drawings and paperwork she had been given at the glassworks.

§ *By the evening of Sunday 6 October, Pile Shutdown Programme No 79 had been drafted, typed, checked, copied, distributed, read, discussed, and agreed. All relevant personnel had been briefed and all requisite systems and pieces of equipment were in place in readiness for the following morning.*

All Shook Up

Hopes that it had been some kind of weekend party passing through were dashed when they emerged on Monday morning. The car park was just as full and there seemed to be just as many people wandering about the streets of the village.

With a terse: "Let's go down to the lake," Charlie strode off across the road, causing several cars to brake sharply. Miranda dodged between them, glaring back at the angry drivers. She hated it when Charlie got like this. She wanted to be angry as well, but knew there was no point. Something deep in the past had done this and it could only be unravelled slowly. Whatever fire burned within Charlie was far less volatile these days. But it was still bloody annoying. So she followed at her own pace.

Up by the Bank, Miranda saw Charlie ask directions and then look around before kicking the stone wall beside her. When she caught up with her, she didn't say anything, simply walked beside Charlie as they headed off down a long road that led, eventually, to the water's edge. There, too, people were milling around. Miranda could see Charlie was controlling herself, like she did on the fairground when idiots cat-called and made lewd comments.

At Thwaites, Charlie asked about hiring a boat. There was shaking of heads and pointing and more shaking of heads. Long-faced she returned to a bemused Miranda.

"I messed it up."

"What? What's the matter?"

"I should have checked and it's only going to get worse."

"What are you talking about?"

"This was meant to be a quiet getaway. Out of season. But it seems Donald Campbell is going to be making another record attempt on the Water in a few weeks and everything else is closing down."

"Oh, Charlie, don't look so miserable."

"It was meant to be a treat."

They had walked away from the water, stood beneath some trees away from the group of earnest young men with pipes and hungry eyes who seemed to infest everywhere they went.

"Don't be sad, sweetheart. We can always come back when it's quieter."

Charlie wanted to sulk again. Normally she would do a spin on the Wall to break her mood. Here, she forced her way out of it.

"Sorry. Didn't mean to grouch. Just wanted it perfect."

She strode off and grabbed one of the earnest young men, dragging him back to where Miranda stood. Miranda bit her lip to stop herself laughing. She'd never seen anyone look so worried. Even after Charlie put her camera in his hands, he looked like he thought he was going to be beaten up and robbed.

"Three or four pictures of us girls together," Charlie ordered, looking round for a decent background. She linked arms with Miranda and the earnest young man did as he was told, before escaping as quickly as he could.

"Useful for something, at least. Other than smoking pipes and keeping people awake."

Miranda, still hooked to Charlie and not caring who saw, kissed her on the cheek. "Let's go find something to eat."

"We can always go over to Ambleside or Keswick for the rest of the day."

"And tomorrow," said Miranda. "Can we go to the seaside? Somewhere quiet. Somewhere to go swimming."

"Be a bit cold and I didn't pack costumes."

"Don't care. We could swim naked."

"And get arrested." But Charlie felt better at the thought and the spark she saw in Miranda's eyes.

§ By 11:45 on the morning of Monday 7 October, the main blowers had been switched off and the control rods were being withdrawn from the bottom of the pile. Withdrawal continued in stages through the day with the shutdown fans being switched off at 14:15. The pile reached criticality at 19:25.

Man On Fire

After another night of people moving and talking and closing doors none too quietly, they came down to the lobby of the Inn to find it completely deserted. With a narrowing of the eyes, Charlie raced back upstairs. Her boots, even though they were muffled by thick carpet, made a satisfying thunder, followed by the slamming of their door. Twice.

When she came back down, she picked up the bike panniers and winked at Miranda before heading out the back. A bleary-eyed receptionist appeared from some inner hideaway and Miranda smiled brightly.

For some reason, the panniers were giving Charlie problems. While Miranda was inside settling the bill, she squatted beside the Shadow in the car park and puzzled it out. It didn't take long, but it still managed to attract the attention of a young man in flannels and pullover, the inevitable pipe jutting from the side of his mouth. She could see him out of the corner of her eye as she reseated the bolt.

"I expect your chap knows he'll have to declinker all the grommets on that before sweating off the widgets," he said with an annoying drawl.

Charlie ignored him with a vague nod. Idiots, she had learned, are best humoured in the first instance, just to see what kind of idiots they turn out to be.

"Don't be an ass, Wickers," cut in another voice. "It looks to me like the young lady could strip down that bike and rebuild it blindfold while you were still working out which knife and fork to use on your breakfast sausages."

Without getting up, Charlie turned her head, fixing the panniers by feel. An older man stood in the shadow of the doorway beyond the other.

"Sorry, Skip," said the young man, playing with his pipe.

"Don't apologise to me. And get rid of that awful green jumper. Won't have it."

"No, Skip. Sorry, miss. Didn't mean any offence." He ducked back into the Inn.

Charlie nodded again, this time with a bit of a smile and turned her attention to the older man. "You've got engineer's hands," the older man said, before she could ask. "They know how a machine works. How it is running. How to put it right." Someone called to him from inside the building as Miranda emerged.

"Watch out for idiots," he said and was gone.

Charlie looked at Miranda. "What are you smirking at?"

"Young lady," said Miranda, suppressing a laugh. "If only they knew."

"He was being polite. You should try it some time. It might suit you. You're not too old to put over my knee."

They were both silent for a moment. Charlie cleared her throat and straddled the Shadow. A swift push of the foot kicked it into life. Miranda climbed onto the pillion and Charlie felt the familiar pleasure as Miranda's arms settled round her waist. She gave them a quick squeeze and then rolled the motorcycle forward to the car park entrance. After a brief pause to let a car pass, the bike was out on the road.

§ *At 02:00 on Tuesday 8 October, the pile physicist went home, satisfied that the operation was going well. The control rods were re-inserted and by 04:00 the pile was shut down. By 09:00 recorded temperatures were either stationary or falling.*

Cumberland Gap

The Wrynose and Hardknott Passes were as much fun as Charlie had hoped. They had left early enough to avoid the bulk of any traffic. One or two cars were struggling with the steep, winding roads, drivers gripping their steering wheels, darting looks of annoyance and envy as Charlie wove past them and roared away.

Curves and sharp bends, sudden ups and downs, the stomach tingling weightlessness of little bridges, all mixed with the roar of the bike. Miranda loved every second, absolute confidence in Charlie.

Eventually the ride was over and they coasted slowly through a village, round a curve beneath a water tower, under a railway bridge and down to the sea.

"If you could turn that into a fairground ride," said Miranda once they had stopped, "you'd make a fortune."

"Will this do?" asked Charlie, pointing toward the sea.

"You're here, aren't you?"

Charlie smiled and started the bike again. To their left a row of houses climbed up a small hill. There were several hotels. At the top they stopped and tried the nearest. It was closed. A second had a sign up saying 'No Rooms'. The third was open and they went into the small hallway, a reception desk tucked in under the stairs.

A young woman appeared. She looked tired.

"Do you have any vacant rooms?" asked Charlie. Miranda was looking at a notice board.

"We only have the one at the moment. Twin beds. Do you mind sharing?"

Charlie turned to Miranda. "Are you all right with that?"

"Sorry?"

"Sharing a room. Twin beds."

Miranda was very good at it now. The barest hint of annoyance. "No. That's fine."

"I'd better warn you as well," said the receptionist, "that there's a lot of 'flu about, just now."

"We both had our jabs," said Miranda. "Last week. Our boss insisted."

"Bet he didn't pay for it," she said with a lowering of her voice and a quick turn of her head toward the office door.

"No," said Miranda, "but we got time off to go and get stabbed."

"Hurt, does it?"

"For a couple of days."

Charlie said nothing. She hadn't felt a thing.

"Why'd she do that, then? Make you get your jabs?"

"We work with a lot of people," said Charlie. "Didn't want us passing anything on to the pun… customers."

"Or us getting ill. 'Flu is nasty."

The receptionist frowned. "You work in a shop then?"

"Sort of," said Charlie. "We sell stuff. Just glad to get away from it all for a week."

A key was produced from beneath the desk. "Room Eight. Up the stairs and then go right to the end of the corridor. Breakfast is between eight and nine. Lunch is twelve to one. Evening meal starts at six."

They climbed the steep, thickly carpeted stairs, their footsteps muffled, and made their way along the dark, stuffy corridor. At the far end, they found a large door with a slightly crooked brass '8' fixed at the point where the mullion and crossrail met. Opposite was a door with a small panel of heavily frosted glass into which was etched the word 'Bathroom'.

The key was loud in the lock, turning with a series of clacks. When the door opened, bright sunlight streamed around them. Miranda ran forwards to the large window.

“The sea!” she said, excited.

“You great soppy,” said Charlie as she closed the door. “You saw it just now.”

“But not through a window. It’s different.”

Charlie shook her head with a smile and put the panniers one on each bed. While Miranda gazed at the sea with her hands pressed to the glass, she began to unpack them.

Later, they walked down the hill, pausing to admire the figure-head fixed to an old cottage perched on the edge of the shore. In the corner shop, a cave of wonders, they armed themselves with magazines, more postcards, a pack of cards, and bought a choc ice each. Charlie dragged Miranda out when she started looking at buckets and spades.

Glad of their heavy bike jackets in the cool breeze down by the water, they walked side by side in silence. They had the beach more or less to themselves. A large, black dog ambled by going in the opposite direction. It ignored them completely. They watched the sharp faced mongrel as it trotted happily through pools and skipped over rocks. Insubstantial in the distance a figure moved with no apparent purpose. Charlie knew it would be the ideal time to ask Miranda, but the moment was so perfect, so calm, just them alone concerned only with stopping slivers of chocolate from escaping, that she was suddenly too frightened to spoil it. Miranda might say no.

§ *During the rest of Tuesday 8 October, the rods were manipulated to keep the pile temperature steady. Reaction was sluggish but gave no cause for concern.*

Too Much

A morning in Keswick and a sumptuous meal did nothing to prepare them for their afternoon visit to the wonder at the summit of the wonderfully named Eleventrees. Beyond the line of houses at the bottom end of the ever winding lane, the views grew broader. Once past the farm and through the embracing tunnel of ivy covered trees, somewhere past the dry stone walls, time dropped away. Beyond the last signs of the modern world, surrounded by the peaks of the distant hills, opposite a wind-sculpted copse of blackthorn where ravens perched, they stepped out into another world.

A chance remark in the pub where they had eaten had sent them there to the small plateau. Thin cloud muted the sun to a broad, almost painful glow; darkening over the hilltops. Leaving the bike on the road, they walked up the slope of the field to where the stone circle stood.

The short path up to the stones passed through wiry autumn grasses, aeons of time, and myriad levels of reality. As they approached, the stones seemed to grow and the gap between them seemed to widen. Charlie saw fluttering shadows ahead of her. Was aware of other figures in some other dimension. Silent winds chased, the skies flickered, strange colours raced in faint swirls across the meadow and between the unchanging stones. It was as if all the days that had passed since the stones were sunk like needles into the flesh of the earth were passing at once.

Miranda was equally captivated, a step behind Charlie, feeling as if she was wading against a flow of water, pushing into a silent wind. The closer they came to the circle the fiercer the winds that tugged at her, the less contact she felt she had with her own small world. The presence of Charlie was a steady beacon on which she concentrated until, without any discernible threshold, they had stepped into an infinitely peaceful sanctuary within the circle.

Round And Round

"I see things," Charlie had once said. It was as far as she had ever dared explain it in the past. Now…

Miranda sat cross-legged in bed. They had said little all the way back from Castlerigg. Were silent through their evening meal. Made little but essential small talk in the evening. They had sneaked into the bathroom together. Even there, the shared experience was one of silence.

"It felt like… all of time was there at once. Like… a mirror that reflected everything. Except me. 'Cos I was the mirror."

She shook her head and looked pleadingly at Charlie for an answer of some kind. Miranda was not a complicated person. Intelligent. Clever. But not complicated. And this had clearly stunned her.

"Is that what it's like for you?"

Charlie grasped Miranda's hand and lifted it to her lips.

"I mean… I'm glad we went." She looked deep into Charlie's eyes. "I think I'd be too scared ever to want to go back."

"Me too," said Charlie almost too quiet to hear, knowing for herself there was no real choice. She could decide to go if she chose, and Miranda had been good reason not to wander. She had, as yet, to discover a way to stop herself being pulled in against her will. "Me too."

§ *In the middle of the afternoon of Wednesday 9 October it was noted that temperatures in the core of the pile were rising sharply. With temperatures in the 400°C range, the inspection ports on the top of the pile and the hatch at the base of the chimney were closed. At 22:15 the four fan dampers were opened to allow air to flow through the core. Temperatures were held steady by this manoeuvre. However, at midnight, they began to rise again.*

All The Way

A sickly haze, lit by a reluctant moon just past the full, clung diaphanously to the fields. Fields as far as the night accustomed eye could see from the top of the embankment. Huge fields. Regular. Divided only by ditches into which the constant rain of sprays drained away. Metal spires struck upwards, transverse branches hung with wire mesh to act as windbreaks now the trees were gone.

Machines moved blindly in the dark. Ploughing, planting, weeding, harvesting. Trundling back and forth along their satellite directed paths. Shadowy monsters grumbling to themselves in the flat, empty landscape.

Empty but for the people where people were not supposed to be, hurrying along access roads, crouching for shelter by mounds of rubble where a village had never been properly cleared. They stayed away from the death traps that were the ditches, where the heavy fumes would suck the consciousness from any living being, slowly dissolving any body that subsequently rolled into the toxic cocktail of herbicides and pesticides they drained, like pus, from the land.

For a while their thin, limping shapes were gone, shadows absorbed into shadow as they rested. Then moving once more, climbing the embankment to where the rails were stitched to the concrete before crossing over and slipping down again into the shadows that bred them.

In the distance, the machines continued to follow their paths. Above, thicker cloud drifted across the moon, obscuring it completely. For a while the low level toxic haze glowed and then that too faded and there was nothing but darkness and the muted sound of the tireless machines.

Turning to go, she was stopped by a bright spark in the night, like a distant, solitary firework, crackling and fizzling in silence as it faded. She watched transfixed, straining her eyes to see if the after images were just that or a dancing string of coruscations growing out of the night. For what seemed an eternity, nothing was certain. Blinking didn't help. The night seemed stubbornly dark, yet something, a faint memory perhaps, or a stray photon triggering an impulse too faint to register as vision acted as an irritant. So, she waited. And waited. Until a faint pattern flowed.

She had no memory of it arriving. It was simply there, as it always had been. A sapphire blue lattice of light both bright and invisible. Fascinated as always, she traced the individual strands as they wove and danced, saw again the blight, the place where the colour had become dull, where the dance had stilled, where the flow was sluggish.

"Are you all right?"

Miranda's voice had travelled a long way through dreams and sleep from the half wakefulness of a warm bed. It reached Charlie who found herself standing naked at the window.

"I'm sorry. I didn't mean to wake you."

"You didn't," Miranda's voice was fainter as she slipped back into sleep. "Come back to bed before you frighten the natives."

Charlie grinned at her reflection in the cold glass before crossing the room. She slid back between the sheets and into Miranda's embrace, strange thoughts and roiling visions left by the window to fade away.

That'll Be The Day

Drawing themselves out of the previous day's dream was difficult, especially for Miranda. It wasn't until they made it down to the beach in the afternoon that their heads began to clear. The dog that had ignored them on Tuesday, ambled by and ignored them all over again. Once it had gone, they were completely alone.

After taking pictures of each other, they walked northward awhile before climbing up off the sand and passing through a tunnel beneath the railway onto a golf course. By instinct they headed away from the brute complex to the north with its steaming cooling towers and top heavy chimneys, the dull steel globe. It shrivelled time, sat leaden on the world.

In the lee of the railway, they wandered back toward the town, gazing about. If anyone was playing golf, they could not see them. Charlie, heart hammering, found courage from somewhere.

"Em?"

Her croak was cut over by Miranda. "What's he doing?"

"Who?"

"Sorry. What were you going to say?"

Amazed at how quickly courage could drain away, Charlie said: "It'll keep. Who are you talking about?"

"Over there." She pointed inland. "Must be a track or something. See that van? That's the third time it's stopped. And that bloke has climbed out and… I don't know. Looks a bit furtive, that's all."

"Must be stealing sheep," said Charlie. "Probably got half a dozen in that van by now. His wife's a demon knitter in need of fresh supplies of wool."

"What's she knit, then?"

"Woolly jumpers for sheep."

§ *Through the early morning hours of Thursday 10 October the dampers were opened four times. Each time the temperature fell, but each time it soon rose again. At 05:10 came the first indication of higher than expected levels of radiation. This was put down to the successive opening and closing of dampers disturbing dust and was not considered hazardous. Just after midday the dampers were opened again and for a sixth time at about 13:30. Radiation in the stack had now increased markedly and by 14:00 there were signs that a release of radioactive material had occurred. As a result, it became evident that something was seriously wrong in the pile. A health physics van was sent along the track to Seascale at 15:00 to take readings as it was feared radioactive material may have been carried from the site.*

After discussion it was decided the likeliest cause of radiation was a 'burst' fuel rod and that the rod should be pushed out of the pile for retrieval once the anneal was complete. At 16:00 a plug was removed to effect the ejection. When this was done it was observed that a number of fuel channels were red hot and that a number of fuel elements had been distorted by the heat. The extent of the fire was determined by removing more plugs. A decision was then made to create a fire break around the affected area by using steel rods to push out unaffected fuel elements. A team of eight donned white suits, full face masks, and gloves.

Another health physics van headed to the north of the complex at 17:00 to take off-site samples.

Although a fire break was created, those elements already alight continued to burn. Just before 24:00, the works fire brigade was put on standby.

I Love You So Much It Hurts

Feeling nauseous and in a foul temper, seething with anger at her own cowardice, Charlie tidied the room in silence. She had left Miranda downstairs to finish her breakfast. When Miranda returned to the room, everything was packed that needed to be packed.

"One last time on the beach?" asked Charlie.

"It's quite cold today."

"Please."

Miranda frowned. She could see Charlie was on edge about something, felt nervous herself as a result.

The beach was deserted. Not even the dog was in evidence. The wind was brisker, blowing off the sea where it had chopped the tops of the grey waves into whiteness.

Charlie tried to wet her lips, tried to swallow the strange taste of fear and still could not find the courage, was close to tears. It was only when Miranda stopped and grabbed her sleeve.

The fear on Miranda's face killed her own. "I wanted to ask you," she said.

Miranda frowned. "What?" It came out as a kind of gasp.

"Shit. Sorry. I had this all planned. Would you…" She rubbed her hands together, palms sweating. "Would you come and live with me if I… we bought a little flat? Just us two."

"Move out of the house?"

"Yes." Charlie was nodding dementedly.

A tear ran down Miranda's cheek before she let out an ear-splitting whoop and danced round Charlie like a wild child, kicking up sand. Finally out of breath she stood bent over in front of Charlie, panting.

"So. Is that a yes?"

Miranda peered up, grinning and crying at the same time.

"I meant to ask earlier, but kept losing my nerve."

"You? Lose your nerve? You ride the Wall of Death. You're Charlie."

"Yes. But this was important."

"Is that why you've been so ratty? I was scared for a moment this morning when I saw your face."

"I'm sorry, Em. I didn't mean—"

"It's all right."

They stood facing each other for a moment, not caring about the chill wind or that it was the end of their holiday.

And then Miranda danced some more before the reality sank in.

"It'll be like being married, I suppose."

They looked at each other again.

"I'm scared. People will know."

"Do you think they don't already?" asked Charlie.

"Yes. I'm sure Daisy does. And the Princesses. And that's all right. And I know one or two others won't mind… But it's not the same is it. What about Dad? Oh. Never mind. We can sort it out later. There's plenty of time. All the time in the world."

§ *In the early hours of Friday 11, the weather changed. A cold front moved south and the light wind that had been blowing from the north east was replaced by brisker, cooler winds from the north west.*

At 01:00, the Chief Constable of Cumberland was informed of the fire. A Most Severe emergency was called and the emergency plan was put into readiness.

With the fire still burning, and all other options exhausted, the order was given at 09:00 for the works fire brigade to pour water onto the pile via hoses fixed earlier that morning. As a result of this there was a large release of radiation that continued for two hours.

Despite water pouring onto the fire, it continued to burn. At 10:00, the cooling fans were switched off, stopping the flow of air to the fire. Almost immediately the fire began to die. By 12:00 the fire was under control and all but out. The Chief Constable was informed the emergency was over. The hoses were left running for the next 30 hours.

The Colour Of Night

Come On Let's Go

"Come on sleepy head."

Whey faced and honey haired, Miranda emerged from her untidy nest of blankets. Charlie looked at the drawn expression and unfocussed eyes.

"Did you have a bad night?"

"Don't think so, 'specially. Just tired. Why's the light on? What time is it?"

"I'll go down and get breakfast."

"Just a mug of tea for me," called Miranda to the empty doorway.

She was heaving herself out of bed when Charlie re-appeared. "Are you sure you're all right? We can put this off to another day."

"Just a bit early, that's all," she said peering at the alarm clock. "We can get a bacon roll on the way."

Charlie paced in the kitchen and hallway whilst Miranda got ready. It was meant to be a big day yet Miranda seemed not to care. But when she finally emerged at the bottom of the back stairs in her bike leathers and an uncertain smile, Charlie's heart melted.

It went even softer when they stepped outside the back door and Miranda cooed with delight at the sight of the dense fog that had settled overnight. The far end of the garden was no longer visible. Daisy's chickens crooned somewhere off to the left beyond what looked like a dissolving fence. The oak was nothing but a pale trunk vanishing into the murk above.

"Are we still going?" asked Miranda as she turned to Charlie.

"I've promised Daisy we'll be careful. And at least it's not like that smog we had a few years back that put John in hospital. You can barely taste this one."

When they emerged from the warehouse it was to a deserted, ghostly street. Charlie wheeled her bike out, glancing across at the wobbly wooden palings that were, optimistically, meant to keep local children away from the last few unfinished flats. More effective was the night watchman who, impervious to cat-calls and insults, would scuttle out of his hut clutching a length of timber if any child so much as breathed on the fence.

They stared up for a moment at the first floor windows of the flat directly opposite the doors of the warehouse.

"When are we going to tell? The builders won't hold the flat forever without a deposit."

"Soon," said Miranda. "This afternoon when we get back. If it's quiet. I want Daisy to know first."

They looked at one another for a moment like scared seven year olds about to face punishment and then laughed.

Charlie climbed onto the Black Shadow and kicked it into life; the throaty purr of its engine muffled even more by the fog. The show bikes were noisy, but that was to give the punters a thrill. Her own bike had been tuned to sing sweetly as she rode. They both waved as the night watchman emerged from his hut and Miranda climbed onto the pillion, hugging Charlie tightly, making the most of the only time she could do it in public.

Travelling westward through London, Charlie took her time. She'd done the journey so many times before that the dense fog didn't worry her. Every junction as it materialised was familiar, every set of road works known. She cut down the south side of Clapham Common, along Nightingale Lane, and down through Kingston until they reached the Leatherhead Road.

By that stage, the fog was starting to dissolve. For long moments everything was lost in a fierce, eddying, silver-grey before vague shapes were limned by sunlight in the thinning vapours. Torn rags of vapour were whipped up in curls as Charlie opened the throttle.

The town centre was still misty but the sun was doing its best to warm the winter day as they cruised through. Out on the site, a large field with a small hangar and sheds, there was little left but a faint mistiness, and they sat side-by-side on the bike to eat the bacon rolls they had bought, drink tea from the flask that Daisy had prepared.

Too excited to sit still for long, Charlie wolfed down her roll and scalded her mouth before striding across to one of the sheds. She unlocked the door and swung it back. Her head down, fiddling with the chain that would hold the door open, she didn't notice Miranda's detour to the bins. When she looked up, Miranda was walking toward her.

"Well?" asked Miranda, half guessing already.

"Close your eyes," said Charlie. "Grab my hand."

Miranda did as she was told and Charlie led her inside. They stood for a moment whilst Charlie's eyes adjusted. Then, gently, she disentangled her hand from Miranda's.

"Just a few more seconds."

As quietly as she could, she crossed to where something stood swathed in a large dust sheet.

"Where are you?" asked Miranda. "This better not be a trick."

"Open your eyes."

There was a silence. "It's a dust sheet," said Miranda with a frown.

Charlie tugged at the corner she had clutched in her hand. The sheet fell away. Revealed was the completed frame, painted to match the others and with the new mirror installed.

Miranda began to cry. "I…" she said. "You…"

"I arranged it with Robertsons to have the mirror sent here so I could bed it in the frame as a surprise for you. You all right?"

"A bit… faint."

Charlie stepped sharply over to Miranda and grabbed her hands. "Into the sunshine with you."

"No. Want to look at the mirror. I'm all right. Just…" She punched Charlie on the arm. And then burst into tears again.

Charlie put her arms around her, kissed away the tears. "I'm sorry," she said in a whisper.

"Don't be. I'm just being stupid. I half guessed. Thought you were just going to show me the painted frame."

They stepped up to the mirror, saw themselves distort in the curved glass, grinning at each other.

"I love it," Miranda said eventually. "And I love you."

Charlie smiled into the mirror.

Witchcraft

They found it quite by accident when they were rearranging the mirrors to accommodate the new one. A way of placing some of the mirrors so that if you stood on a certain spot, you couldn't see yourself in any of them, yet you could see what seemed to be a reflection of the mirror behind you. It was just a matter of angles. They measured it all out carefully and reproduced it in Miranda's trailer. Charlie moved the mirror fixings and bolted a square of steel chequer plate to the floor so punters would know where to stand to make themselves disappear.

Even though Charlie knew it was an illusion, it still unnerved her to stand in the centre of the circle of mirrors and not be able to see herself. The few times she did it, she had to spend time in front of the plain mirror to re-attach herself to the world. Miranda, on the other hand, spent a lot of time there.

Fever

"Let me help with—"

"You stay put," said Charlie as she stripped the damp sheets from the bed. "Don't get chilled."

Miranda smiled weakly. She pulled the blanket tighter around herself even though she was still damp and radiating enough heat to steam up the windows of their small van.

"Mattress is OK," said Charlie once she'd bundled the sheets. "Question is, are you?"

Miranda shrugged. "Embarrassed more than anything."

"Don't be daft," said Charlie softly. "Fancy some tea?"

"Ice cream, more like."

"Shame that Mr Whippy van doesn't stick around. There's still some orange squash left."

"OK."

"Then we'll get that t-shirt off you."

Miranda grinned even though she ached all over. "I wouldn't get too close. Might be 'flu or something."

Charlie watched her yawn and then handed her a glass of squash. "Don't drink it all. I'll see if we've got any aspirin left."

“The bottle’s in the small locker.”

Charlie opened the little cupboard next to the sink and in the dim light from the single bulb found the bottle she was looking for. When she turned, Miranda was standing and, with some effort, pulling her long t-shirt up over head. Her hair cascaded down over her shoulders and she twisted to stop the blanket she had been wrapped in from slipping the floor.

Charlie gasped and Miranda turned back to face her. “What’s the matter?”

“That bruise. Turn around again. How the hell did you get that?”

“What bruise?” asked Miranda.

Almost black, it ran right across the small of Miranda’s back. Charlie touched it gently with her fingertips, felt the heat of Miranda’s body even though she stood naked.

“Your poor back. How did you…?”

“I don’t know,” replied Miranda as she tried to look over her shoulder and then under her arm.

Charlie opened a drawer and pulled out a hand mirror, holding it so Miranda could see her reflection in the long mirror on the door.

Miranda began to cry. Slow tears. “I don’t know.”

Charlie threw the mirror on the bed and, scooping up the blanket to wrap it round Miranda, held her close.

“No need to cry, sweetheart.”

“It’s horrible.” She sniffed back more tears. “The only thing I can think is when I lean against the rail by the booth when it’s not busy. Haven’t done it for a few days.”

“Does it hurt?”

Miranda shook her head.

“No more leaning back on that rail then. I’ll see if I can fix one of those flip down seats for you.”

“Promise you won’t tell Daisy.”

“Em.”

“I don’t want her to worry.”

“And it’s all right if I do? All winter you’ve had colds. You’re not eating properly. No. Don’t give me that look. I’ve noticed. So I’m not making that promise.”

Charlie combed back Miranda's hair with her fingers, kissed her still feverish brow.

"For now, madam, back to bed."

Miranda did as she was told without argument. Which worried Charlie more than anything else.

Breathless

They ran the finale, three bikes on the Wall, to the accompaniment of heavy rain. It hammered the canvas canopy and they could see spectators holding hands over their ears at the onslaught of noise. The rainstorm continued after they brought the bikes down.

"We might have to close if water keeps getting in," said Beth as she grabbed a rag and wiped moisture from the centre floor.

All around them drips began to descend. They all looked up to see the canvas roof sagging with the weight of pooled water.

"I'll go up with the broom again," said Charlie. "Push the water off."

As she headed for the door, Lorna and Beth pulled a tarpaulin from its shelf under the centre box and began to cover the bikes.

In the booth at the front, Mary sat staring at the rain with a glum expression. On a normal day she would be shepherding people off the Wall so she could start letting the next lot of spectators in. Today she didn't have the heart.

She and Charlie sighed at each other as Charlie reached in for the long-handled broom.

"Nobody's moving," said Mary. "Gallopers are at full stop so people can shelter. All the sideshow tents are crammed."

Charlie peered out through the gloom. A lone rumble of thunder elicited squeals from youngsters. Hunched up figures scurried for whatever cover they could find.

"Going to be another flamin' washout," said Mary.

Charlie wasn't listening. She had glanced in the direction of Miranda's show, watched as a family braved the rain at full tilt, heading for the steps, only to change direction. She would have thought no more of it, assumed that the maze was full except for the lone figure that ran up the steps, tapped on the glass of the booth and got no response.

"Must be inside," said Charlie to herself.

"What?"

When another family tried to get in, Charlie forgot about the broom, grabbed Mary's coat, and slung it over her head before squelching across the muddy turf, fighting to keep her balance on the slippery ground.

There was little relief at the top of the steps as the rain was blowing every which way. Charlie went through the entrance using her key. The door was normally opened by a pedal inside the cash booth by Miranda or whoever was on duty. Inside, the working lights were on and a number of people dripped, children making the most of their time in front of the mirrors. There was no sign of Miranda or anyone else from the fair.

By the exit, behind the last mirror was a black painted door that gave access to the booth. You had to know it was there. Charlie used her key again, but the door seemed to be stuck.

"Em?" she called in a hoarse whisper.

There was no response and she pushed harder, putting her eye to the slightly wider crack. In the gloom, beneath the stool, a body lay curled.

For long seconds as rain thundered on the roof, Charlie did not know what to do. Her heart in her mouth, unable to call for help, she bundled Mary's coat up and wedged it in the door so it wouldn't close again and then went stumbling out into the pouring rain to get help.

I'm Sorry

Grey ripples danced across the ceiling, first one way and then another. Miranda struggled to focus on them and then wished she hadn't so she closed her eyes again and began to drift back to sleep. In that warm limbo a wave of despair hit her from one direction just as a consciousness of what had woken her arrived from the other.

Fighting back up from soft darkness, scared in case she had imagined it, she lay as still as she could between the starched sheets and listened. And there was the voice. Somewhere beyond the door. Angry and urgent. Distant and getting closer.

"You should be… No fit state…"

"Already knows…"

"Needs quiet…"

The door to the side ward opened a few inches and the voice was suddenly clearer.

"What she needs is what you and your staff cannot give her right now."

Charlie's face peered round the door, eyes searching. She saw Miranda, tried to grin and managed to wink before she withdrew.

"And I see there's a spare bed in there with her, so if I've got to—"

The door was pushed wide and Charlie stepped into the room followed by the Ward Sister. A dozen emotions fought for Charlie's face and all yielded in the end to the tears as she stepped across to Miranda, leaned down and held her close. The door closed with a soft shush.

"Is it visiting time already?" Miranda asked, her voice soft and slurred.

Charlie disentangled herself.

"No." She couldn't say anymore.

"Don't cry."

"I can't…" She found a handkerchief.

"How did you get in? Was that the argument?"

"I'm so sorry, Em. It's all my fault. If we hadn't gone—"

"Don't. No. Not ever. It's not your fault."

They looked at each other and Charlie spoke before they both started crying again.

"I have to have tests as well. Because we went to the Lakes together. In case it was that accident at the power station. We were both there. Together."

Miranda struggled to stay awake. "They doped me up. I didn't handle it well."

"Nor did Daisy. I got torn off a very wide strip for not telling her sooner you were ill. But I thought you'd got better. And there's that drug, Mercaptowhatsit, they're going to give you. You'll be better in no time."

"No. Don't. The doctors told me everything in the end."

"But you're going to take it?"

"Can you imagine Daisy if I so much as thought of refusing. But it's so far gone we all know what the chances are. So don't try to comfort me with lies."

"I'm just so angry. So… useless. But I promise, Em. I'll not lie to you."

"And yourself. Promise me you'll never lie to yourself. God. I'm so scared. Just love me."

"Always, Em. Always."

Twilight Time

Black metalwork came and went as they passed through the Kingston Gate into Richmond Park. The run up from Brighton had been reckless with Charlie gunning the bike to 102mph just south of Crawley. And then taking to back streets because she thought she'd seen a police car. Egg and chips in a road house. Refilling the tank. And despite the humid weather and darkening skies, giving in straight away to Miranda who just didn't want to go home straight away.

Just inside the gates, Charlie turned off Queen's Road and cruised slowly up Dark Hill to start a circuit of the park. By the time they had come back round to the Isabella Plantation, the heavy sky had taken on a greenish tinge. The bike purred into silence and they eased themselves off, removing their helmets and wiping their brows.

Miranda's eyes were still wide with the exhilaration of it all, alive as they hadn't been in the months since she had learned she had leukaemia.

"Daisy must never, ever hear about that," she said, perching sideways on the saddle as they looked southward down the hill.

"No fear. Not from me."

"And thank you."

"For what? Putting you in danger?"

"Don't start that again or I'll get cross. And I don't want to be cross. It's too hot for one thing. For taking me to Brighton. For going so fast. I never thought I'd have the courage, let alone enjoy it. You gave me that."

In the distance the city had disappeared into a darkness that flickered.

"Someone's copping it," said Charlie and shivered as the sound of distant thunder reverberated through the hot, flat air.

Nearby several deer lifted their heads.

"Is that coming this way?" asked Miranda, edging a fraction closer to Charlie.

Several people came striding out of the plantation and climbed into a car, eyeing the southern horizon.

"It's been following us up from the coast," Charlie replied as the car pulled away. "Doubt we'll get home now without getting soaked."

"Let's stay then. Watch it. We can sit over there."

Miranda nodded toward the building behind them with its roofed porch as other people drove away in the flickering gloom. Charlie wheeled the bike as close as she could and they stepped into shelter as the heavens opened. Hail pounded down, drowning out the growing and continuous rumbles of thunder.

When it stopped it was relief to their ears. Short lived. The rain began in earnest, smashing into everything and pouring off the roof above them as they huddled as far back into the shelter as they could. The ground disappeared as puddles grew and joined, streams began to flow down the trackways in the grassy slopes.

Eventually the rain eased off to a normal downpour but the sky, now dark as night, continued to be torn with lightning, crazed baskets of light woven across the heavens, flickering sheets of pale blue, of orange, of pink, and yellow backlighting dark and ever changing cloudscapes. And all the time thunder, loud and soft, assailed them where they stood in shadow.

When the rain finally stopped and the sky went dark and quiet, Miranda turned to Charlie, squeezing the hand she held.

"I'm glad I was here for that," she said and Charlie wept.

Pulling Down

It Doesn't Matter Any More

Cool, sweet air suffused with the scent of ancient books filled the dim, narrow spaces of the shop. Crammed onto seemingly endless shelves were volumes that waited patiently for a new owner. *The Grasshopper Lies Heavy* by Hawthorne Abendsen passed beneath a fingertip, but did not jump out. *The Grave on the Water-Front* enticed, but she'd read other Bendrix titles and didn't think it would be right.

Charlie had been sent home weeks before. The others had kicked her off the Wall. She hadn't been concentrating properly. There hadn't been any accidents. Not even a near miss. But they knew she needed to be in London with Miranda. So they'd put it to the vote and given Charlie her marching orders.

It had been a strange send off. They had ridden up with her in convoy. To make sure she got there safely, they had said, but she knew they all wanted to see Miranda and she had greeted them where she lay in bed. Charlie had warned them and they kept their faces cheerful and kept their tears in check until they were back downstairs in the kitchen where Daisy filled them with pie and mash before seeing them off again. Miranda's lorry had long since been garaged at Leatherhead and her mirrors were neatly stacked in the warehouse.

Idly, Charlie picked up a copy of *The Oak Tree* by Orlando Shelmerdine, leafed through, and nearly put it back. At the last moment she changed her mind. Perhaps for later. So she added it to the other books she had chosen, a couple of Rex Wests and a fantasy adventure called *The Sleeping Sword* by J C Cutwood.

Next came a long line of titles by William Barclay and James Colvin that she had already read. She wondered briefly what it must be like to sit at home all day just writing. They must be strange people, she concluded, but was grateful for their efforts nonetheless.

She passed over *The Furrow* by Stephen Johnson, a *History of Crome* by Henry Wimbrush which really should have been in the non-fiction part of the shop. Another that caught her eye was *One Human Minute* by J. Johnson and S. Johnson. She looked inside and hastily put it back when she saw the copyright notice was for 1988.

At the end of the shelf, just past a Rosie M. Banks titled *Only a Factory Girl*, was a volume that chilled her blood and left her shivering. A dark green volume. Near the top of the spine, embossed in silver, were two vertical lines – I I – and at the base a spiky wheel made up of eight arrows.

Her hand was on the volume, ready to pull it from the shelf when she let go and backed away, suddenly angry. Hot tears flowed on her cheeks. It could stay there, she thought. And rot. What earthly use was it to her? It would not tell her anything she did not already know and it could not help her go back, to save her Nan, to save Miranda.

The Day The Rains Came

Daisy had fallen asleep. A warm breeze had strength enough to stir the half drawn curtains, fill the room with summer. Charlie checked her battered Record watch, saw she was back before she had promised. Back down in the kitchen she made a pot of tea, moving with practised stealth. The whole house had become a place of peace. At any other time it would have been wonderful. Miranda was always moaning about the noise the little ones made as they sped around at their games. Now Charlie would have given anything for them not to be banished, for them to be shrieking up and down stairs and racing about the garden, getting told off by Daisy.

She lifted the rumbling kettle from the hob and poured, stirred, rattled the lid into place.

Daisy appeared. "She's still asleep," she said with a tired smile and lifted the pot to pour.

"How much tea did you put in this?"

Charlie looked down at the still open caddy which was now half empty. Unshed tears blurred her vision.

"Go upstairs. I'll make a fresh pot. And Charlie?"

Bewildered, Charlie looked up as Daisy wrapped her arms around her.

Upstairs, Charlie stood in the doorway of the room for a moment, still conscious of Daisy's kiss on her brow. The air was suffused with the subtle scent of honey and the sweetness of summer flowers, the warm breeze still stirred the curtains. There had been a storm the night before. Growling thunder. Heavy rain. Perhaps for the first time in her life, Miranda had slept all the way through. She slept still.

Sunlight caught the bevelled edges of the dressing mirror, painting a vivid rainbow on the wall. Sapphire sparks drifted through some other room, some other place, before fading. Charlie shivered, febrile in the torpid dreamspace. The room where it all began. Where it all must end.

Hardly able to breathe, she stepped lightly across to the bed and lowered herself into the chair where they took turns to keep watch. Miranda still slept and there was nothing more Charlie could do. She looked around at all the familiar things, but there were no answers, no miracles. I am become dust in the sunlight, she thought, a helpless ghost in her fevered dreams.

Daisy brought in fresh tea that wasn't the colour of pitch and a plate of freshly cut sandwiches. Charlie thanked her even though she rarely felt like eating any more. She sat staring at Miranda who was ravaged by both the disease and its failing cure, dying now and sleeping in a morphine haze.

How can that possibly be you? she thought. There and not there. Already gone and still breathing. Goodbyes already said in case there is no other chance. So full of life. So fragile. Broken beyond repair. Travelling beyond reach, even of me. The sweetest of flowers doomed from the very beginning.

To keep the black at bay, she reached out with a foot and hooked her bag toward her to look at the books she had bought. *Alice* was still on the bedside table with a marker at the place she had reached reading it to Miranda. Beside it, the old Victorian chess set, one queen on its side, the other missing.

Without looking into the bag she pulled out the volumes that had been tied together with string and put them on her lap.

Where the strength came from to stay seated, to keep quiet, to keep from ripping it to shreds, she did not know. How it came to be there. She did not know. The green volume with its silver wheel. She wanted to scream at the universe to leave her alone, to tear it down to a smoking ruin, to push it into the deepest frozen waters.

The haze left her eyes and she was still sitting with the books in her lap, tired to her very bones. With careful, silent movements she stood and crossed the room, pushing the unwanted book into her trunk. When she got back to the chair it was to see Miranda watching her.

She nearly broke at sight of the pain wasted face and patchy hair, cut short, the deep shadows about the eyes as if darkness sought a way within only to be constantly denied its prize by the fierce light already there. Where the strength came from to smile Charlie did not know. But smile she did, crooning softly as she damped the piece of sponge in its bowl and held it to Miranda's mouth. The clouds in Miranda's eyes cleared for a second and she smiled back, her deathly pale countenance relaxing for a moment to allow a younger Miranda to shine through.

May You Always

The room was unfamiliar. Their room. Pale light from outside lit the ceiling and upper walls with angular blocks, like winter in summer, daytime at night. The bed was wrong, narrow and neat, positioned with its head beneath the window, its foot toward the centre. Beyond it, a plain desk and chair, a chest of drawers, a narrow wardrobe. She stood immobilised, knowing it was wrong, not knowing how.

The light outside came from a single lamp several stories below. It stood beside a path crossing a grassed courtyard. Close beside it, an elegant aspen shimmered in the night. All around, dark windows looked back.

She stepped back from the wide window and moved with silent steps around the bed. A cone of light from a lamp on the desk that had not been there before fell across papers and a pen. Moving toward it, she heard a sound and stopped. Turned her head to look at the bed.

Sleeping with a clear, relaxed face was a young girl with pale honey coloured hair. Just a few feet away and impossible to reach. Sandalwood and rose scented the still air.

As she stood in calm contemplation of the peaceful face of the sleeping child, a soft arrhythmic sound teased her senses. Too soft to be a scratching, too hard to be a hiss, she tried to pin-point its source and realized with a chill that it came from just behind her.

All lost at the vicious barking of dogs, the thrum of engines and a great shadow through which the faintest of ghosts played, singing in silence, dancing without moving, watching the stone skitter its way to sky blue. Standing in a dark space surrounded by the cold, stiff, dark cocoons that would one day butterfly into being, a bright microcosm of light and sound, the crazy piping of the gallopers organ, the sirens and laughter fading to a small, brightly painted ghost train car where she sat side by side with a fading reflection. She tried to grasp her hand; was left with nothing but a fading smile.

Summer lightning lit her pain with faint, sapphire light and she saw herself reflected in dark glass – staring, strained. With a sudden movement, she sat back and found herself in the chair beside Miranda, sunlight flashing from the blue of the sapphire she now wore openly on her hand.

In that same hand she held the book she had been trying to read. With care she closed it and placed it on the bedside table with Miranda's copy of *Alice*. Perhaps there would be another day when it didn't seem such a terrible sacrilege.

Glowing in the same sunlight, Miranda's pink sapphire ring was still on her finger, the skeletal hand resting with ethereal lightness on the bedsheet. Ever since she had come home from hospital she had insisted on wearing it, placing it on her left hand ring finger. Some thought she was confused by the morphine. Charlie knew better.

Lost in thought, she did not see Miranda wake, did not see the slow progress of her hand, knew of it only when she felt the gentle touch of trembling fingers on her own ring, pulling.

Charlie frowned, but she slipped the ring from her finger and let Miranda hold it.

"Other hand," whispered Miranda.

For a moment Charlie did not understand, befuddled by grief. And then she knew and slid her left-hand ring finger round to where Miranda held the blue sapphire, let her push it on as far as she could manage before helping her finish. They sealed their marriage with a kiss and Miranda, exhausted, slept.

Sleep Walk

Beneath the tree it was still raining, an intermittent patter of cooling drops upon her upturned face. She was feverish with exhaustion and stood awhile in hopes of relief. Within the embrace of its ancient breathing stillness, within the aegis of its long dream and the happy times to which it had borne witness, Charlie merely felt small and alone. The rain did not wash the tears away.

Banished, she had traipsed out into the garden on some now forgotten impulse. It was vibrant in the early morning, refreshed by the rain, bright with colour, awash with scent, basking in the early warmth of the busy old fool. A blackbird, perched on a nearby shed roof, made love to the new day with its song. Charlie's song was of a breaking heart and she looked around with eyes that did not really see. She had not been this tired in half a lifetime, not since the bombs had stopped falling.

She looked at her breakfast in much the same way, leaving it uneaten on the kitchen table before hauling herself up the back stairs. It was a weary journey, step by reluctant step into inescapable shadow. At the top, she nearly forgot herself, turning to the right to go to her own room.

A moment leaning against the passage wall as the deep, dark weariness threatened to overcome her, and then turning away, passing the landing cupboard, stepping through layers of vision that unfolded like the petals of a black rose, seeking out Daisy's room and the makeshift bed there.

It had been neatly remade and she sank down on top of the covers, was asleep before she even had time to worry whether she would. Deep asleep and darkly dreaming.

Petite Fleur

Long since dry, the path was hot beneath her feet. She stepped off and crossed the lush grass toward the rose beds, fussing at the damage, pruning away battered blooms and dropping them into Alice's old trug.

Bees sang sleep in the garden, a warm breeze the seductive chorus. Charlie listened and felt the deep aching tiredness inside beg for relief. It would be easy to sit down on the bench beside her or, better still, go right on to the end of the garden and lie down on soft grass in the shade of the oak. There she could dream of the days they had played and run free, dream of the days when there was a future, of the days…

She stepped round the bench to the rose bed that had been Old Tom's pride and joy, second only to his vegetables. There were new bushes there now, added several years before by Charlie, and she sought out the best blooms on the new plants. A large, light-pink old garden rose called 'Miranda' with tightly curled inner petals nestled in a bowl of larger ones. And a light yellow shrub rose, its outer petals faded almost to white, that bore her own name.

Holding the thorny stems lightly in her left hand, she returned to the house and the cool of the shady back stairs. It was all a dream now, so many memories assailing her at once, climbing through the archaeology of her own life, of those other lives and places, of the laughter and of the tears.

The air in the room was immediately suffused with the subtle sweetness of freshly cut roses. Charlie lowered herself into the chair. There was nothing more to be done.

On the bedside table, the newly filled glass vase stood waiting. The yellow and pink roses were forgotten in Charlie's left hand, the thorns dimpling the flesh of her palm. Her right hand had reached out and was curled around the hot, parchment-dry flesh of a starved hand that curled itself around hers.

The knowledge that no matter how long Miranda survived she was, in effect, already dead was a terrifying pain. The wasted fingers clung to her own. Each slow shallow breath was an imperceptible struggle against entropy in the fading daylight, each gentle lift of the bed clothes marking one step closer to the end, mesmerising, yet doing nothing to calm Charlie's raging interior, the screaming self that wanted to envelop the fading spirit and hold it fiercely that it might never slip away, knowing all the while it was an impossible thing to hold, knowing that it may well have slipped away already away from the pain, free of a broken, dissolving body breathing its last few seconds away. And yet, the fragile hand still held hers, her thumb gently caressing the fevered dry flesh, willing Miranda to know she was not alone, she was loved, desperately loved.

The faint squeeze startled Charlie and she looked up from her misery to see Miranda had woken, was smiling, was already drifting back to the darkness. Her eyes closed. She was gone, had slipped away so that the whole of her was now fragmented, haunting the inner worlds of all those who loved her. Still there perhaps. A ghost. But never again able to dance in the sunlight of a new day.

Around her, Charlie felt the silent witness of ghost children who had gathered, caught a glimpse of a rose garden where the roses bloomed as dark as midnight. Realised that Miranda no longer held on, no longer breathed. Charlie leaned forward and kissed the lips that were, for the first time ever, unresponsive to hers. The mirrors in her mind shattered in a blinding cascade, thousands of lightning-bright razor-edged shards tearing her heart to ribbons. Her left hand tightened about the rose stems, numb to the pain of the thorns piercing her flesh.

The Storm Has Just Begun

Daisy heard Charlie come down the stairs and glimpsed her through the kitchen window as she walked away from the house.

Something in the set of her, the way she carried the two roses in her left hand, was all she needed to know.

Wiping her hands on her apron she raced up the back stairs and stepped into the sunlit room. Peace had stolen gently into Miranda's hollow face. The tight lines of pain, deep etched for so long, had ebbed away forever. Her hand was relaxed. She had always been heart-liftingly beautiful, even through the nightmare months when disease had eaten at her. But now the child's face had returned – not a care left in the world. Daisy sat beside her and let her tears flow.

Later, when they searched for Charlie, she was nowhere to be found. They searched all night and all the following day: every room, cellar, corridor, garden, shelter, and shed along the street; in and beneath every bed, behind every door, in every cupboard and chest, and, because it was Charlie, on every rooftop. And when they had searched them all again, they spread to the surrounding streets and alleys and knocked on every door.

All they found was the trail of droplets of blood from where the thorns had pierced her palm. They marked her route down the back stairs, through the garden and along the packed earth of the alley. They could be seen in the dim light of the old warehouse, leading across the concrete floor to Miranda's mirrors.

One of them had been uncovered. She must have stood there a while because a little pool of black spots stained the ground in front of the mirror. Of Charlie, though, there was no sign. But when they later cleaned the floor, some flaw in the mirror made it seem as if the trail and pool of blood were still there, disappearing into the reflected universe beyond.

Notes

Each chapter takes place during a succeeding year. Their titles derive from the following sources:

Setting Up (1945) – the fairground term for constructing the rides and sideshows on a site.

Ich Will Kein Engel Sein (1946) – German for 'I do not want to be an angel'. It echoes what Charlie says in 'Declarations', the third chapter of *Thin Reflections*.

How Like A Winter (1947) – from Sonnet 97 by William Shakespeare.

How like a winter hath my absence been
From thee, the pleasure of the fleeting year!
What freezings have I felt, what dark days seen!
What old December's bareness everywhere!
And yet this time remov'd was summer's time,
The teeming autumn, big with rich increase,
Bearing the wanton burthen of the prime,
Like widow'd wombs after their lords' decease:
Yet this abundant issue seem'd to me
But hope of orphans and unfather'd fruit;
For summer and his pleasures wait on thee,
And thou away, the very birds are mute;
Or if they sing, 'tis with so dull a cheer
That leaves look pale, dreading the winter's near.

The Old Wound Now Forgotten (1948) – from the lyrics of 'White Room', written by Pete Brown (music by Jack Bruce) and performed by Cream on their 1968 album *Wheels of Fire*.

Dark Ride (1949) – A dark ride is the name for any fairground attraction that involves punters being taken into an enclosed environment, like a Ghost Train.

Fair White Wings (1950) – from: "Those who have learned to walk on the threshold of the unknown worlds, by means of what are commonly termed par excellence the exact sciences, may then, with the fair white wings of imagination, hope to soar further into the unexplored amidst which we live." – Ada Lovelace

Rust Upon Iron (1951) – from: “Guilt upon the conscience, like rust upon iron, both defiles and consumes it, gnawing and creeping into it, as that does which at last eats out the very heart and substance of the metal.” – Robert South (‘On the Danger of Presumptuous Sins’, in *Sermons Preached Upon Several Occasions* (1727), Vol. 3, p. 291.

The Last Degree (1952) – from: “The American, English and French newspapers are spewing out elegant dissertations on the atomic bomb. We can sum it up in a single phrase: mechanized civilization has just achieved the last degree of savagery.” – Albert Camus, *Combat*, 8th August 1945. Although the specific reference is to Charlie’s nightmare (at the moment the UK tested its first atomic bomb in the Monte Bello Islands at 00:59:24 on Friday 3 October) it also relates to the murder of William Albert Bonwick, alias Potato Pete.

The Ravell’d Sleeve (1953) – from: *Macbeth* (Act II, Scene ii) by William Shakespeare.

Smile Of Light (1954) – from the poem ‘Summer Night’ by Bryan Waller Procter (the pen name of Barry Cornwall) in *The Poetical Works of Barry Cornwall*, Palala Press, 2018. The relevant part of the stanza is: ‘Oh, the Summer night, Has a smile of light, And she sits on a sapphire throne…’

My Midnight Pillow (1955) – from: “What terrified me will terrify others; and I need only describe the spectre which had haunted my midnight pillow.” Mary Shelley on the writing of *Frankenstein*.

All That Calm Sunday (1956) – from: ‘The Golden Voyage to Samarkand’ by James Elroy Flecker.

The Ninth Anneal (1957) – refers to the operation that took place at Windscale Pile No 1 to cleanse it of Wigner radiation. It was during this operation, the ninth of its kind, that the Windscale fire occurred on 10 October 1957 releasing radiation to the atmosphere and surrounding countryside.

The Colour of Night (1958) – from: ‘Lightning hides the colour of night’, one of a number of ‘Six-word Stories’ to be found in *To Evince The Blue* by Munia Khan (Xlibris, 2014). It is used with kind permission of the author.

Pulling Down (1959) – the fairground term for dismantling the fair at the end of its time on a particular site.

The subheadings of each chapter are titles of songs popular in the particular year in which the chapter is set.

www.ingramcontent.com/pod-product-compliance
Ingram Content Group UK Ltd.
Pitfield, Milton Keynes, MK11 3LW, UK
UKHW041826200726
13854UKWH00002BA/586

9 781909 295155